"What are you doing in my house?"

Maeve waited impatiently for his reply. "Well, Mr. Sherbert? I haven't even had breakfast yet."

"Neither have I." He chuckled. "And it's Corbet. Ash Corbet. Breakfast getting is hard on a bachelor. Why don't you whip up something tasty for both of us?"

"I'll whip you," she muttered.

"Uh-uh-uh," he warned, shaking an index finger at her. "You did promise—is someone still on the phone?"

"My mother," she gasped. "And long distance, too!"

"Start fixing breakfast," he ordered, brushing by her to pick up the phone. Her blood began to boil—then he was back again. "You go talk to her."

Maeve rushed for the phone. "Mother!" She growled her indignation over the wires.

"He sounds very nice," her mother returned placidly from the other end of the line. "Very nice. How does he look?"

EMMA GOLDRICK describes herself as a grand-mother first and an author second. She was born and raised in Puerto Rico, where she met her husband, a career military man from Massachusetts. His postings took them all over the world, which often led to mishaps—such as the Christmas they arrived in Germany before their furniture. Emma uses the places she's been as backgrounds for her books, but just in case she runs short of settings, this prolific author and her husband are always making new travel plans.

Books by Emma Goldrick

HARLEQUIN PRESENTS
1035—IF LOVE BE BLIND
1087—MY BROTHER'S KEEPER
1208—MADELEINE'S MARRIAGE
1281—A HEART AS BIG AS TEXAS
1360—LOVE IS IN THE CARDS
1465—SILENCE SPEAKS FOR LOVE

HARLEQUIN ROMANCE
2967—THE LATIMORE BRIDE
2984—PILGRIM'S PROMISE
3111—THE GIRL HE LEFT BEHIND
3134—MISSISSIPPI MISS
3164—A TOUCH OF FORGIVENESS
3188—DOUBLY DELICIOUS

Don't miss any of our special offers. Write to us at the following address for information on our newest releases.

Harlequin Reader Service
P.O. Box 1397, Buffalo, NY 14240
Canadian address: P.O. Box 603,
Fort Erie, Ont. L2A 5X3

EMMA GOLDRICK

Smuggler's Love

Harlequin Books

TORONTO • NEW YORK • LONDON
AMSTERDAM • PARIS • SYDNEY • HAMBURG
STOCKHOLM • ATHENS • TOKYO • MILAN
MADRID • WARSAW • BUDAPEST • AUCKLAND

Harlequin Presents first edition September 1992
ISBN 0-373-11488-5

Original hardcover edition published in 1991
by Mills & Boon Limited

SMUGGLER'S LOVE

CHAPTER ONE

MAEVE McCORMAC came out onto the tiny back porch of the old cottage and stretched in the sunlight. Hers was one of some thirty houses scattered haphazardly across the edge of the beach at Smugglers Cove. They were all built in the nineteen-hundreds when the railway came across the Florida swamps to Cedar Key. Years later, when the rail line was moved south to Tampa, Smugglers Cove and the surrounding little settlements were practically abandoned.

Now the Cove consisted of worn houses, gray with fatigue and only half of them inhabited, and a general store. The whole settlement was perched on a tiny bit of beach facing the Gulf of Mexico. Behind it to the north the Suwannee River swamp extended for miles. One dusty dirt road went south to the even more isolated village of Cedar Creek. Another went east across the swamps to the higher land of North Central Florida. They, and an ancient telephone line, were all that connected the Cove to civilization.

"But it's all mine," she told the dog. Beowulf was an overage and overweight wolfhound. Well, almost a wolfhound. His mother had boasted a pedigree two miles long; his father had come from a good neighborhood. The dog's muzzle was gray with age; he matched the houses. But every now and again he could be stirred to violent things. Just at the moment he was too busy sniffing long-forgotten smells. Fresh air from the Gulf of Mexico, that tangy sea-air, filled with clam smells as squalling sea gulls dropped their prey on the rocks to open the shells.

The dog stood three feet high at the shoulder, almost a match for his mistress who managed a mere five feet from head to toe. The toe being bare on this early June morning; the head covered with a close cap of auburn curls that clung tightly. Almost as tightly as her old T-shirt clung to her full figure. Men whistled when Maeve walked by, which was why she had taken up judo at an early age. Besides, except for one minor aberration, she loved her computer more than she loved people in the world, and trusted her machines more than all the men she had ever met!

And now it was men again. She was angry enough about her so-called uncle. Angry and tired and confused, but determined. This property at Smugglers Cove was the last piece of her not inconsiderable inheritance still available to her. And now a crew of men were hard at work on the breakwater.

"Not that I have anything against men," she instructed Beowulf. "On occasion I understand they can be very useful. But..."

These particular three men were working on the old stone sea wall that separated her segment of the beach from the land of whoever it was that owned things to the south, around the edge of the hill. The breakwater stretched out into the water a good fifty feet, running parallel to the rickety wooden pier, the only one visible at the Cove. Having only arrived on her new acres late on the previous night, Maeve had no real idea just who her neighbors might be. Or why the men were going to such trouble to tear down *her* wall. So, holding tight to Beowulf's collar, she ambled down the grassy strip in front of her house, out onto the sand, and over to stand behind them, watching.

"That must be hot work," she offered after a suitable time. Two of the men turned to look.

"Go 'way, kid," the oldest one suggested as he turned back to the labor.

"Damned hard," the younger one said. He was young enough to see the woman rather than the "kid." "We thought it was a dry-wall construction. Turns out to be cemented together. Might have to get the bulldozer over."

"Must be some important reason for tearing a wall down," she said in her mildest tone. Beowulf padded his lines by growling at them all. The dog had a massive, an awesome growl. All bluff, but the men could hardly know that. Neither Maeve or Beowulf wanted to advertise the fact that the big animal had flunked out of the Canine Corps because he was too kindly to bite!

Maeve remembered that discharge scene vividly. She had come down to Fort Benning to reclaim her animal. "Cowardice," the military police lieutenant had fumed. "Drummed out for cowardice. Refusal to bite. Like that." At which point Beowulf had ruined the scene by biting the lieutenant on the leg before towing Maeve out of the headquarters building with a military policeman in hot pursuit. And now, far away from Georgia, the dog was at it again.

"Jeez, he don't bite, does he?" The work stopped as the three men moved in what they thought was an inconspicuous fashion, over to the other side of the wall.

"Bites all the time," Maeve assured them mournfully. "His father abused him when he was just a child—puppy, I mean. Never got over it. Gets along with women all right, but... You were saying about the wall?"

"Well, can't rightly say," the older man said. "Mr. Stanley says to come and take it down, so we come to take it down."

"Mr. Stanley?"

"You must be new around here," the young man added. "Rob Stanley. Owns all the land for a mile or so south and around the cove. Got him that fancy house around on the other side of the hill. Lives there with his mother, you know."

"Well, a man who takes care of his mother can't be all bad. I guess maybe I'd better get to know him." Maeve's laughter was a low chuckle that attracted attention from man or beast, but mostly man; although she herself was unaware of the fact, it was blatantly sensual. "Suppose one of you runs over to tell Mr. Stanley I'd like him to come and see me?"

"You got to be kiddin'," the older man said. "We got work to do. I can't imagine—what you just said. Mr. Stanley, he don't go to other people. They come to him. Hat in hand, if you please."

"Do you think my hat will do?" Maeve doffed her big straw Mexican hat and tried to restore the two artificial hawk feathers to more pristine beauty. Come on, her conscience nagged at her. They're only working slobs. Don't run this thing into the ground!

"Nothin' wrong with your hat, lady, just your mouth. Mr. Stanley don't like smartmouths. Now, if you'll just go away, we'll get back to work."

"I think you ought to consider my message," Maeve insisted. "Especially since it's *my* wall you're tearing down! Now, if you don't quit this vandalism I'll have to set the dog on you. Mr. Stanley?"

"Oh, Gawd!" For a moment the three of them stared at her, but when Beowulf made a sudden readjustment to pouncing position they backed away, picked up their tools, and disappeared around the edge of the hill.

"Easier than I thought," she told her dog. "Or maybe that's just the start of things." She tugged at the dog's collar and headed back up the hill. Beowulf gave a good imitation of the Terror of the West, and then meekly followed. When they arrived back in the grassy little plot that fronted the house, Maeve plopped herself down, yoga style, and looked around.

Her thirty-five-foot motor home, all gleam and gold, was parked against the side of the house. In fact, it looked as if the house were leaning over, resting on the vehicle. "Might take a heap of fixing up," she told her dog. Beowulf yawned. So did Maeve. Yesterday's drive had been ten hours long and her air conditioner had blown out. But, after four years of living on wheels, she badly wanted a fixed residence—at least for a time. So thinking, she fell gently backward in the grass, and in moments the pair of them were fast asleep.

Rob Stanley came up on them entirely by surprise as they lay in the grass, surrounded by the dainty pink and white glory of rose gentian. The little girl was sprawled out in a buttercup sundress, a huge straw hat over her face. The dog was stretched out at her side with a baleful eye open as Rob nudged Saracen to a halt. The horse shied away a couple of steps before Rob could rein him in. The dog silently opened his mouth to display a serried row of very large teeth. Rob grinned at the dog from his vantage point high in the western saddle, but his humor turned to amazement as he scanned the girl. She had squirmed on to one side, her skirt riding up to display magnificent thighs, firm full breasts outlined by sun and shadow, a narrow waist blooming into pattable hips. The dog growled.

"I'm not running a peep show. Perhaps you could ride off my property?" A dark-timbred contralto, with just the slightest touch of sarcasm riding on it. His eyes snapped up. The straw hat had been pushed back an inch or two, and one gleaming green eye stared at him as Maeve propped herself up on one elbow.

Rob started to swing down out of the saddle, but the dog convinced him it wasn't a good idea. The animal stretched to its feet and moved closer to his stirrup, that huge mouth open like an invitation to the arena.

"Your dog——" Rob fumbled for words, something almost impossible to believe of one of the important development specialists on Florida's west coast. "Wolfhound?"

The hat fell back as the girl sat up. The movement allowed her dress to fall back, releasing the tension at her breasts and hips. Almost as if by magic she seemed a little girl again. White skin, and a line of freckles across her nose. Auburn hair, close-cropped in a mass of curls, surrounded her pixie face. She tugged at the hem of her dress, her head tilted up as she looked him over, one hand raised to shade her eyes from the brilliant sun.

"Partly," she said. "Wolfhound, crossed with Tasmanian Devil."

"Impossible," he snorted. "Oh, you're suggesting that your dog is—mean?"

"Stating a fact," she replied. "Very mean. But that won't bother you, since you're just riding off, right?"

"Actually I came over for a purpose," he said. "My men tell me that you stopped the work on my breakwater. My name is Rob Stanley." He extended a hand in her direction.

And *that* caught her attention. She scrambled to her feet and crammed the big hat back on her head. Enter the villain, stage left, she told herself as the wheels in her very clever head spun madly and a youthfully innocuous expression spread over her face. So this is what Attila the Wall Destroyer looks like. Not as old as I had expected. About forty, probably. And not the least bit shriveled or worn. In fact, he's quite attractive, even with that paunch building at his midriff. But I suppose so many girls have told him so that he believes it himself! She smoothed out the expression on her face. It was one of her most important attributes, this ability to look like "little girl lost" while her very efficient brain was at work.

"Yes, I believe there's some misunderstanding," she told him, not moving an inch to take the hand he extended downward. "As it happens, it's *my* beach and *my* breakwater, Mr. Stanley."

He recovered with aplomb, grinning as he inspected his hand for leprosy spots. "I wonder what your friends call you?"

"I don't have all that many friends," she said firmly.

He smacked his lips and grinned again. "Your mother and father?"

"Neither is available," she said. "Perhaps we could settle your problem between us?"

"Just being neighborly," he drawled. "It seemed the thing to do. Maybe I was wrong. Do you mind if I ride up to the house and speak to your mother?"

Maeve was unable to hold the scowl; the grin that replaced it lit up the neighborhood. She snapped her fingers. Beowulf moved to her side, standing poised for a charge if required, his eyes more on the man than the horse. "I don't mind if you ride to see my mother," she said, "although I think it would be hard on your horse. It's a long way to Apalachicola. That's in——"

"I know where it is," he interrupted sharply. "We don't seem to be communicating on the same frequency, little girl." He pushed his Stetson to the back of his head. She maneuvered out of the sun to get a good look at him. A solid six feet tall, probably. Sandy hair, bleached lighter in spots by the Gulf sun; not at all as thick as one might expect. A square sort of face with a prominent jaw. Sharp blue eyes astride a Roman nose. And a crinkly sort of smile that was just the slightest bit attractive. He wore a thin Hawaiian shirt, comfortably faded jeans, and a most expensive pair of boots. Lawyer or used-car salesman, Maeve reflected to herself. Neither one rated very highly in her personal estimation. A man to be treated with some caution!

But there's no need to tease him any further, she lectured herself. Your mother would give you a hard time if she learned about your outrageous behavior. "My apologies, Mr. Stanley. Why don't you come up to the house and have a cold lemonade with me? Freshly squeezed this morning."

He winced at the lemonade part of the offer, being partial to strong drink, and then grinned. Very attractive. Be careful, Maeve! she warned herself. "Do I get to dismount without being attacked?"

"Oh, not to worry." She giggled. "Beowulf is very friendly, just as long as I'm smiling and holding his collar. Come along."

"The kitchen is the only room in the house that's clean," she told him a moment later as he trailed her through the battered screen door. "I got in late last night. I don't expect I'll get to the rest of the place for a day or two."

"Yes, well, that's what I wanted to talk to you about," he said. She cleared the table and fetched a glass of juice from the refrigerator. "My men working on the sea wall said that you said——"

"That it's my wall," she interrupted. "Yes, that's what I said."

He gulped at the drink. "And I suppose you've traveled a long way to get here?"

"Reasonably far. From New Orleans, actually."

"Then I'm afraid I have some bad news for you."

Ah, here it comes, she told herself. Big man has bad news for little girl. To be delivered solemnly and with compassion, right? Maeve mustered up a suitably concerned face, settled herself primly in the chair opposite him, and then turned the screws on with a tiny wistful smile. He was perspiring fairly heavily. She folded her hands and waited.

"The truth of the matter is that I bought all that section of beach and the pier some three days ago," he said. As expected, solemnly and with compassion. Lordy, he's good at it, Maeve told herself. Either he's one great actor, or he really means it! Since honesty was something Maeve seldom came across in her day-to-day life, she tried to look behind his mask for cracks, and found none! So there was nothing left for her but to play it straight.

"I'm sorry to hear that," she said. "From Shamus McCormac, I suppose?"

"Why, yes. A friend of yours?"

"I don't think so. In fact I'm pretty sure he isn't. You bought the entire estate?"

"Not exactly," he assured her. "I wanted to buy the entire Cove property, but he was only interested in selling off the pier area. He did say that he might come back this way, and, if the deal for the houses wasn't done, he might entertain my offer. I have the papers right here."

Maeve scanned the document he presented, doing her best to keep her lip from twitching. It was the same as all the others. Uncle Shamus's sprawled signature spread across half the page, and, under his name, the typed title, "Executor of the Estate of M. McCormac."

"Wait here just a minute." She sighed as she got up from the table. "Stay, Beowulf. Would you want some more lemonade, Mr. Stanley?" He shook his head negatively. "Stay, Beowulf," she repeated, and was off to the side door, out into the motor home.

The papers she wanted were hidden behind her stack of computer materials in the bedroom of the van, which she had converted into a business office. She found the document, but wanted a moment to think. The upholstered passenger seat accepted her weight. She patted the worn arm affectionately. For years, and for fifty-nine thousand one hundred miles, the immaculately kept vehicle had been home to her restless spirit, and a place of business as well, and she treasured it.

Rob Stanley was as much a surprise to her as she to him. But then, not entirely a surprise. She had followed the trail of "Uncle Shamus" for the past four months, all the way from the Texas panhandle to this last enclave in backwater Florida. And now she was only three days behind him! She sat back and closed her eyes, picturing the man who claimed to be her uncle. A round butterball of a man, he was described as, full of laughter and light and lies. No one had a picture of him, this man who had filed a false death certificate for Maeve McCormac in four separate states, and thus wiped out her credit cards, her Social Security identity, access to her bank accounts, and even her driving license.

Then, using a fake will, he had gained control over most of the widespread property she had inherited when she was only ten years old, and sold it off at bargain prices to people accustomed to shady deals. The man who had legally wiped Maeve McCormac out of existence. Him. Everything gone, except for a few things she still held around Apalachicola—a small bank account, the family house where her mother still lived, and whatever she might make with her magic touch and her computer terminals. And Smugglers Cove, which she was *not* about to give up.

After four months of trailing just behind him, sweet, naive Maeve McCormac had turned herself into the Baskerville hound. She had come to Smugglers Cove ready for one devil of a fight. And here was her first opportunity! She fingered the paper on the chair beside her. A fine work of art, purchased in the stews of New Orleans. As fine a forgery as money could buy.

How would handsome Mr. Stanley react? She could hardly forget elderly Mr. Wilson, of Tallahassee, whose first reaction was to punch the little female who was disturbing his deal. That was the trouble with "Uncle Shamus." He sold only to people with sceptical pasts and irritating futures. Not a nice man among the lot. Oh, well, face the music.

Stanley and Beowulf were staring at each other when she walked into the kitchen. "I thought I'd stretch my legs," he reported. "Your—dog thought otherwise."

"He'll do better when he gets to know you," she assured him. "*If* he gets to know you." She slid into her chair gracefully, adopting the same solemn expression and tone *he* had used. "Mr. Stanley, I think I have some bad news for you."

He caught the innuendo. A frown swept over his face, and suddenly he wasn't very handsome any more. "Why do I get the impression that someone here is about to cause trouble?"

"I wouldn't know," she replied. She ducked her head and spread the legal paper out in front of her like a card-sharp selecting the winning ace from a crooked deck. "You'll recognize the paper, I'm sure," she offered. "It's a bill of sale for all this property, made out to me, signed by one Shamus McCormac, executor of the will of the late M. McCormac, and dated March 15th."

His hand came across the table cautiously, as if he expected something to bite. "You have to be kidding." His face flushed as he turned the paper over. "You've got to be kidding."

"Not me," she assured him. "I'd never do a thing like that." Her chair was too tall for her. She squirmed around, trying to get comfortable, while he took the paper and read it. Or seemed to read it. In fact he concentrated only on the date and nothing else.

"Damn," he muttered. "Crooked as a snake's belly. I *knew* he was up to something." He slapped her paper back down on the table. Beowulf growled.

"I believe so." Maeve sighed and settled back into her chair. "But oh, so valid. Where do you suppose he is, this Shamus McCormac? At the moment, I mean?"

"I don't know," he growled at her, "but I'll find out. Believe me, I'll find out."

"And then you can sue him," she offered happily.

"Sue him? I'll—oh, no, little lady," Stanley said. "You I'll sue. Him I'll—have my friends take care of." He pushed his chair back and climbed to his feet. "My lawyers will be along in the morning," he snapped as he made for the door, ushered out by Beowulf. No more sunny smile, no more "handsome is as handsome does."

Just a very angry large man, who intended to do something about something.

Not about me, Maeve prayed. She had become cynical in the past few months, but not all that brave. Not all that brave at all. And Mr. Stanley was so angry that, after he'd swung up into the saddle, he roweled his horse unnecessarily with those gleaming spurs and galloped away across the saw grass. Maeve tapped gently on her forged bill of sale, and took it with her to the door, where she shaded her eyes to watch Rob Stanley dash off. The poor man had been so angry he hadn't even noticed that there was no name on the paper showing to whom the land had been sold. Well, after all, a girl could hardly think of *everything* in this confusing world. If she didn't have a name she could hardly enter it on a legal document, could she? But surely his lawyers wouldn't be that blind.

"Mr. Stanley left just a little bit put out?" Another male voice, almost at her side. Maeve whipped around, hiding her paper behind her back.

"Yes, I believe he was a little—disconcerted."

"Then let me welcome you to Smugglers Cove. My name is Corbet. Ash Corbet. I'm the unofficial mayor around these parts."

Her reaction was automatic. Not yet the actress she needed to be, she put her little hand in his. "I'm——" she started to say, and then clammed up. She had already given too much away by telling Stanley that her mother lived in Apalachicola. And now *this* one. Younger than Stanley. Not at all handsome. Well, perhaps that wasn't exactly true. Tall, thin, a whippet of a man rather than a bully. A brush of dark brown hair, with a cowlick that seemed to perpetually threaten his right eye. A pair of jeans that looked as if they had seen better days. Big dark eyes—soulful eyes. Eyes that seemed to see through one with no trouble at all.

"Ima?" he questioned.

"Er—yes. I'm called—that by some people."

"Ima," he repeated. "You don't look like an 'Ima' to me."

Her temper flared. It had been a bad day all around. "So, what are you," she snarled at him, "some sort of psychic?"

His grin was disarming. "No, just some sort of painter," he said. "Not a very great sort, you understand. Smugglers Cove is half squatters and half struggling artists. You look more like a 'June' to me. Local joke. Not very funny, huh?"

"Not very," she told him glumly. "But then nothing seems very funny these days."

"Listen," he continued. "I know it isn't the polite thing to say when we've just met, but you be careful of your dealings with Mr. Stanley. He still thinks he's the boss of the plantation."

"You don't have to warn me," Maeve said. "He's only *one* of my problems."

"Want to tell me about it? I'm a good listener."

And he obviously was. She almost fell into that same trap again. She badly needed someone to confide in— but this one could hardly be the one. "No," she sighed, "when I decide to confess I'll find a priest. Or a police lieutenant."

"Curious mixture," he said, chuckling. "Well, Ima, I came along to welcome you, and to invite you to the weekly Saturday night do over at the community hall. Country music and refreshments." He turned and took a couple of steps, then came back.

"Priests or police, huh? That's not the only kind of solace to be had."

"Please," she sighed. "Please. I don't need any cheering up. I'm twenty-six years old, I enjoy being depressed, and I'm as good as dead already." And bit her lip. She hadn't meant to say anything like that. It was too close to the truth!

He closed the distance between them. "Life's never that bad," he said softly, and put his arms around her, gently touching her lips with his own. Something soft and gentle was happening. Something smelling of aftershave and lilacs and masculinity. Something just teasing enough to prevent her from gathering her senses. Something warm and tantalizing, drawing her out of herself. It seemed to go on for a year or two, but that could hardly be. She was sure of *that* part of it at least, because when he put her gently back on the porch floor she started to breathe again, and it was her first breath since the whole thing had started.

"Why you rotten——" she started to say.

"Not dead," he commented solemnly. "Definitely not dead. I'm not sure about the twenty-six. I guess I'll need a couple more samples."

His hands came up in her direction, shocking her back to attention. She scuttled away until her back was at the wall of the house. There was an old hammer lying on the porch rail, almost rusted to pieces. She picked it up. "Not on your ever-loving life," she muttered. "Beowulf! Get out here and defend me, you mangy mutt!"

Her dog came, protesting. When tempers flared, Beowulf would rather be smelling the roses. And two tempers were doing *something* he wasn't familiar with. "Now you'd better get out of here," Maeve threatened.

But she could see he already had Beowulf's number. And maybe my own, too, she thought breathlessly. Unconsciously her empty hand came up and scrubbed her lips.

"It won't come off." He grinned at her and reached for his hat. "When I brand a critter the mark never comes off. I *will* go. I wouldn't want to have to fight off your animal. I hope you'll come to the dance."

"You'd *better* leave," she threatened, waving the hammer in his general direction.

"Be careful there," he told her. "The head of that hammer's loose. If it comes off you'll——"

"I don't need your advice, Mr. Almighty Corbet. Just get out of here, and don't come back, Mr. Corbet."

"I'm going, I'm going. You needn't scream at me, Tiger. But I'll be back, little Ima. I'll be back." It all sounded like a threat, but he was laughing, a large joyous laugh that could be easily shared by dozens.

He tipped his hat and strolled around the corner of the house. As soon as he was out of sight, Beowulf barked sharply half a dozen times to display his courage in combat. The noise startled Maeve out of the daydream she had been enjoying. The dream about orange blossoms and children and long summer nights, and things of that nature. The hand holding the hammer dropped to her side, the steel head fell off, just as he'd predicted, and bounced off her toe. She yelled bloody murder. She could hear him laughing from somewhere down the path, and her little fists doubled in the agony of not being able to pound him lustily about the head and shoulders!

Her next caller arrived just after three. The sun, as advertised in all the Florida brochures, had been up and bright all day, and was just reaching the shady side of one hundred degrees. Maeve, tilted upside-down on the front seat of her van, her head deep under the console at the fuse panel, had finally managed to get the air conditioner working. A streak of grease spotted her left cheek, her hair was buried beneath an old baseball cap that said "Portnoys Plumbing," and her stained T-shirt and ragged shorts were a match for each other—both faded red, and both too tight for her compact little figure.

So, when the knock was repeated for the third time, and a hesitant cracked voice enquired, she pulled herself up out of the mass of wires and yelled, "Come in!"

"I be in, but you ain't," the voice complained. Wearily Maeve wiggled her way out of the van and in through the adjacent side door. Her visitor was a wizened old man, slightly bent, totally bald, and standing hardly more than her own height. But he had a smile ten miles wide, and about fifty percent of his own teeth.

"Packy Schultz," he introduced himself. His hand was gnarled, and tough as tanned cowhide. "Live down the road, I do. Seen your van last night. Been comin' to the Cove for nigh on to fifty years. Ain't seen you before." Pause, demanding an explanation. Maeve giggled.

"You don't sound like any Florida cracker I ever met," she teased.

"Come from the North," the old man said doggedly. "Lived in the Bronx when I was young. Back when people could live in the Bronx." He pronounced it "Bronnix."

"Packy?"

"Nickname," he allowed. "From a long time ago. My—associates and I—we were in the—moving business. So I was called Packy."

"Makes sense," Maeve agreed. "Can I offer you anything?"

The old man's face lit up like a fireworks display. "Wine," he said quickly. "Rothschild 07."

"I'm afraid I don't have anything that swift," Maeve told him, and watched as the smile froze.

"Around here somewheres," the old man mumbled. "Gotta be around here somewheres."

"I don't understand," Maeve said sympathetically as she pulled off her cap and shook her head. All those lovely auburn curls fell into place instantly. "Please— sit down, Mr. Schultz. You look a little pale."

"Been away," he admitted as he sank into the chair. "Been away. You don't know much about the Cove, I s'pose?"

"Not much," Maeve admitted. "My—er—uncle— looked the area over some forty years ago. Brought me along for a visit some time later when I was—oh—six years old. All I can remember is the beach and the sea. He meant to develop it, but for some reason put it off...and then he died and left it—I mean, I bought it all from the estate. Try some lemonade?"

The old man made a face. It seems to be the habit around here, Maeve told herself. First Stanley, and now Schultz. Surely they must all drink *something*? But the old man had manners. "Don't mind if I do," he allowed, and took a cautious sip at the sparkling cold liquid.

"And cookies?" The brownies were still warm, having come out of the oven only a few minutes earlier. One of the two things that Maeve could do in the kitchen. Bake brownies and boil water. Packy Schultz grabbed at them, as if afraid she might pull the plate away, and stuffed one in his mouth. Beowulf, who had fallen asleep inside the van while Maeve had worked, stumbled into the kitchen and sat beside the table in the position where the most crumbs might fall.

Silence reigned.

"Good," the old man finally managed. "Folks ain't much for cookin' around these parts. Mostly them artsy folks, you know. Painters, musicians. One or two of them ain't bad."

"Just so they pay the rent," Maeve teased. Packy's face turned a mottled red, the veins of his face standing out as blue streaks here and there.

"Ain't been a lot of rent collectin' these last six months," he told her. "Squatters' rights, that's what most of us live by. You aimin' to throw us all out?"

"Not particularly," Maeve said, smiling. "But I *do* have to eat, and I *do* have to collect some rents. Tell me about the Cove, Packy."

"Not much to tell lately," the old man said. He shifted his weight in the chair painfully. He was so thin that there was hardly a bit of flesh for him to sit on. "But back in the thirties, well, you know—Prohibition, and that?"

"Good Lord!" Maeve exclaimed. "Smuggling? Smugglers Cove?"

"T'aint funny. All true. Used to bring them French and Danish liquors in from the islands, you know. Cigarette boats on dark nights——"

"But there's only one road out of here," Maeve said. "The Suwannee River swamp cuts off everything else!"

"Ain't no reason why the stuff couldn't go out through the swamp on pirogues." The old face had divided itself up into ten thousand crinkles as he smiled at her. "No big deal in them days. We used to——"

"*You* used to, Packy? Good Lord, how old are you?"

"Eighty-six," he said, chuckling. "Wouldn't believe it, would you? Yeah, I was on a lot of them. Did the movin', I did."

"Of course," she replied, laughing. "I thought you meant furniture moving! It must have been exciting!"

"Was indeed. Especially that last trip. Them revenoers finally caught wise. A big fight, there was. Tony Espaldo and his gang. They was caught on the beach. Funny thing, that."

"Funny thing?"

"That whole last load," the old man said, sighing. "Fifty thousand dollars' worth of French wine. And nobody ever found a bottle. It must still be here in the Cove somewheres, but people has searched and searched for years, and never found nothin'."

Maeve sat back in her chair, her eyes wide. She might never be a great engineer, but she understood arithmetic. "Fifty thousand," she mused aloud. "Think how much that would be at today's prices!"

"Jus' think," the old man said. "That's why I been comin' back to the Cove real regular, every time I get out of the slammer—I mean——"

"I understand what you mean, you old reprobate," Maeve said. She looked the old man over. Someone to confide in. Someone who could help? What could be better than a man who had seen the inside of the slammer more than a time or two? Send a thief to catch a thief? Why not? She grinned at him.

"Packy," she mused. "Has a meaning, I suppose?"

"Better believe it," he responded. "Back in them days there wasn't too many guns around, you know. So every gang had some young kid just to carry the weapon. The cops took it easy on kids in them days. 'Juvenile offenders,' they used to call us. Only got caught twice, I did. Judge put me on probation both times. 'The packers,' the fuzz used to call them.''

"Ah—packer. Packy!''

"Well, I was young," he said, sighing. "And a mite stupid.''

"And that's what took you to the slammer?''

"Oh, well, that, and a dozen other stupid things," he confessed. "Ain't got no more of them cookie things?''

"There might be a few," she teased. "I was saving them for Beowulf, but——''

"Don't wanna do no dog outa his supper, but——''

"But I can make him something more, Packy. Interesting profession. Is that what you've done all the rest of your life?''

"Didn't last long," the old man muttered. "Slowed down too much, and then the gangs started usin' females as packers, and—well, that ain't been my main line of work these past fifty years.''

Maeve poured him another lemonade and watched, entranced, as his jaw moved up and down. "Your main line?'' she probed.

"Ain't never been inside because of my main line," he boasted. "I'm a penman.''

"A what?''

"A paper hanger." He gave her a sorrowful look and shook his head. "Don't you know nothin'?''

"It appears that I don't," Maeve agreed. "Penman?''

"A forger," he chuckled. "One of the best in the business. Except for my arthritis slowin' me down, I can copy anything.''

"Can you really?'' Maeve's eyes opened wide, and a smile danced on the corners of her mouth. Manna from heaven! God *does* provide!

"But now," she continued, "you're concentrating on this wine?"

"Got to," he cackled. "Ain't got forever, you know. And you can never tell about wine. It might be bottled gold, or it might be vinegar by now."

"What you need is a helper," she stated firmly. "Someone who could look around for you, and ask questions. A partner."

The old man looked at her suspiciously, then nodded his head and drained his glass. "Might be just the thing," he replied. "Partners. Seventy-thirty split."

Maeve, who knew a con when she heard it these days, smiled. "Sixty-forty," she suggested. "My sixty."

"Oh, no, you don't," he objected. "Fifty-fifty?"

She paused long enough to make him think she was debating the subject. "I guess I could go for that," she returned. "Fifty-fifty split, and I'll throw in a good supper?"

That seemed to do it—the mention of a good supper. "No steak," he said. "Ain't got enough teeth for good meat these days."

"No steak," she agreed, and leaned forward across the table.

"Funny thing," the old man said before she could get another word in. "You bein' young and good-lookin' and all, makes a guy ask just what's in it for you?"

"Mr. Schultz," she said, coming right to the point. "Partner. I have this problem."

CHAPTER TWO

ONE of the Great American Truths was that nobody died at a summer resort. People might stop breathing and make the great jump from artist to specter, but, should that occur, the remains were quietly shipped back "home," wherever that might be. As a result, Smugglers Cove possessed no cemetery.

But eleven miles down the road, at the little settlement of Cedar Key, there was a church, a cemetery, and a bar room. It took Maeve a good hour to convince Packy Schultz that the bar could wait while they sauntered through the tiny graveyard.

"I jus' have this feeling," Packy grumbled, some two hours later. The thermometer had climbed steadily under a cobalt sky. One or two sea birds circled at a distance, hovering over a small motor boat and its fisherman occupant.

"Probably arthritis," Maeve told him, feeling not the slightest bit sympathetic.

"How about this one? Charity Curtis. Born in the same year you was—died before she was three years old." The tombstone was not as ancient as some, but the carving was already weathering away.

"I don't know," Maeve said, sighing. "I know it's suitable, but—suppose you were the mother of the real Charity, wouldn't that make you feel bad to know someone else was using her name?"

"Can't make no omelet without bustin' a few eggs," Packy grumbled. "You got some other candidate?"

"How about if we use my mother's maiden name?" Maeve suggested. "Mary Kennedy. She has no other living relatives, and she won't complain about this." She looked over at the old man scratching his head.

"Somethin's watchin'," Packy grumbled as he came over to stand beside her. "I kin feel it in my bones. Eyes on us, somewheres."

Maeve stretched and made a quick search of the horizon. The cemetery occupied the side of a small hill, with a screen of trees separating it from the road and the town, but leaving it open to face the sea. "I don't see anything," she said, sighing. Working with Packy Schultz was obviously going to be a bigger problem than she had anticipated. "There's some guy out there fishing, but he can't possibly see what we're up to." And then, a little puzzled, "Just what *are* we up to?"

"Nice stone," the old man rambled on. "Mary Kennedy? Why not? I told you a dozen times, partner. You need a birth certificate. One that's foolproof. One that the law can't break. So, as of now, you're Mary Kennedy. You know where she was born, and when? Write it all down here for me. Ah, out-of-state. Nothin' better. Nice. Let me jus' copy this here stuff, an'—you sure there ain't nobody watching?"

"Nobody but the sea gulls," Maeve assured him. "So—you make me a birth certificate. Wouldn't it be just as easy to ask my mother to send *her* certificate?"

"Wouldn't do," the old man grunted as he laboriously copied information into his notebook. "Writ on old paper, it would be. Easy to check up on. An' have the wrong date, and things like that. Nope, invention's the best; everything invented so there's no loose strings to trip us up. Born in Georgia, you say? There'd be too much work for them local bureaucrats to check. They just ain't interested in corr—corr...?''

"Correlating?"

"The very word. Them bureaucrats jus' ain't interested in—what you said there. C'mon, let's get out of here. I'm getting nervous spasms."

Me too, Maeve thought, as she loaned him one of her strong young arms and led the way back to the highway. Packy's old Volkswagen started up under protest. He reached into the side pocket of the door and pulled out a battered silver flask. Both he and the car ran better after the drink. Maeve had wanted to bring her motor home, but had been assured that nothing was more visible than a big golden van driving down the dirt road that hardly strayed fifty feet from the ocean. Besides which, had she moved the van out away from the house, the latter structure might well have fallen down.

As they drove away northward along the narrow road, stirring up a trail of dust, the birds they had disturbed in the cemetery came back to chatter at them, and at the boat offshore.

And at Ash Corbet, sitting in that boat. He tucked his new binoculars away in the leather case, folded up his fishing pole, and tried to crank up his outboard motor. It started after innumerable attempts and half a hundred well-chosen words. He turned his battered little craft north, bumping across the placid waters of the Gulf at flank speed. Which was why Maeve and her partner were back in Smugglers Cove a good hour or more before Ash Corbet picked up his mooring at the north end of the settlement.

He went searching for his pair of targets, but had little luck. Ten or fifteen citizens in a row wanted to talk to their pseudo-mayor, and could not be shaken off. He scouted out the woman's house, but all the doors and windows were shut tight, with not a whisper of sound leaking out. Disgusted with himself, he stomped back down the path to his own ramshackled house to complete his notes.

"And so now all we hafta do is enter your new name," Packy whispered as he leaned over the kitchen table, drawing pen in hand, tongue between his teeth, and created magic. "Mary Kennedy. Jus' let me get the end of this curlicue just right. There—whatcha think?"

"Magnificent." Maeve breathed a sigh of relief. Her forged bill of sale now contained, in the finest Spencerian calligraphy in the world, her new name, emblazoned to perfection. Now, if Rob Stanley's lawyers came through the door prepared to fight, at least she had *one* thing going in her favor. But she still had a raft of doubts.

"You're sure about this, partner? The name?"

"Law says you can call yourself anything you please," Packy advised her as he put the drawing pen carefully back in its leather case. "As long as you ain't out to cheat somebody, that is."

Which I certainly am, Maeve told herself grimly. Several somebodies. And obviously, by the way he was grinning at her, her ancient partner knew exactly what was going on. She shrugged her shoulders. "And now what?"

"Well..." Packy eased himself to his feet, flexing his fingers. "Damned arthritis. Could ruin a man's trade, it could. What now? I think I'd better get back to my shack. I got a couple of them birth certificate forms——"

"From Georgia?"

"Nope. From New York, to tell the truth. I'll fix all that up tomorrow. I gotta soak them overnight in weak tea—for the aging, you understand." Maeve, who did not understand in the slightest, stared at him. "Well, you wasn't born yesterday," he grumbled. "Can't expect to produce no brand-new certificate. Makes no sense. Bound to've got folded in a time or two, turned a little yellow, acquired a few creases. That's what soakin' does. Tomorrow I'll change it to read Fulton County, Georgia, and deck it out with all your vital statistics. That's what they call all them numbers and things. Tomorrow morning."

"Fulton County? That's not where Mary Kennedy was born."

"Not so far's I know, she wasn't. Happens to be the county where I spent six months in the slammer. Not to worry—partner."

"Oh, I won't," Maeve said, sighing, wishing it were true. She was very much worried indeed, and had been for almost two months.

"An' you start thinkin' about where that wine might have got to," he directed.

"Yeah. Sure." She walked him to the door, peering out through a crack to be sure the coast was clear.

It was a sunny afternoon, but Maeve couldn't appreciate it. There was a pay telephone at the general store, and her experience had been reconfirmed. Without a valid Identification Card, the telephone company was not about to come out and hook up her telephone. So she stomped back down the weathered stairs and hunched herself in a corner, her head resting on her arms. The skirt of her bright yellow sundress swirled around her and settled like petals from a buttercup. Beowulf mourned in her ear and did his best to lick her tears away. It was some comfort. She put one arm around the big animal, looking for cheer. It came, but from a surprising direction.

A massive thump beside her shook the worn treads. "No crying in public," Ash Corbet said casually as he sat down beside her. "Prohibited. State law. I forget the number of it."

"Oh, shut up," she snapped. "You're all I need today. First the telephone company, and then you! Don't you have something important to do? Elsewhere?"

"Of course I do." One of his fingers tilted her chin up. She sniffled and scrubbed her eyes with one knuckle. "This is my day for rescuing fair maidens. Any fool can see I'm hard at work. C'mon now, look up here. There's a good girl."

"Oh, shut up! If I feel like being miserable, I will be. I don't need your advice. And I'm not a good girl!"

"Ah. Which, he wonders, does she deny—the 'good' or the 'girl'? Interesting."

"Oh, shut up!" she repeated, but her heart was losing the argument, and it was hard to keep her lips compressed in a straight line.

"That's better." One of those huge arms draped around her shoulders. Beowulf growled. "Oh, be quiet, dog. I'm hugging my girl."

She looked up resentfully. "Don't talk to my dog like that. I am *not* your girl."

"We'll talk about that later. Now, what's the matter?"

"You wouldn't believe my troubles with the telephone company," she sighed.

"I'll believe everything," he replied. "I make it a practice to believe two impossible things before lunch every day. Lay it on me. What makes the telephone company a bigger villain than I am?''

"It's very confusing." She stopped to nibble at her lower lip and run her fingers through her hair. "I seem to get it all settled in one place, and it pops up in another." He was a good listener, she noted. Keeps an interested look on his face, but says not a word. So I might as well tell him, mightn't I? "Look, I *have* to have a telephone."

"*Have* to?"

"I knew you wouldn't understand!"

"I will, just as soon as you explain." He turned his attention to Beowulf. The old dog managed to sit and wag his tail at the same time as Ash Corbet's big fingers found that sensitive spot just behind his ears.

"Lack of money is the root of all evil," she misquoted dolefully. "I make my living as a consultant for companies with computer problems. Only, if I don't have a telephone, I can't contact them. And the telephone company won't accept my—references or anything!"

"That *is* a problem, little Ima."

"And that's another thing," she confessed. "I—just made that up. My name is Mary Kennedy." He chuckled as if it were all a great joke. For a moment she felt like hitting him—but he was so darned big!

"I've dealt with wills and probate and clients," he continued. "I'm really a part-time lawyer by trade. But telephones? Are you sure that anybody's out there waiting for your call?"

"There are a lot of companies glad to get my services," she huffed.

"Doing what?"

"I told you. I'm a computer doctor. I write programs for corporations who can't do it for themselves. I examine existing programs that aren't performing correctly. But I need a telephone so *my* computer can talk to *their* computer."

"Complicated," he mused. "So how do you expect to get paid?"

"An old-fashioned system called cash," she told him. "They send money by United Parcel Service. Even strangers get attention when they have cash in hand!"

"Of course they do." He looked down at her for a moment, lightly touched the curls at her forehead, and stood up. "But one tends to think you might have come to the Cove for other reasons, Mary. I love that name. Old-fashioned."

"I wouldn't say I'm *hiding*," she added cautiously, "but there's a multitude of people who want to sue me. Maybe I need a lawyer?"

He grinned, and refused the gambit. "I'll take care of the telephone company." He stretched to unbelievable height and went gracefully up the stairs. Maeve turned to watch and was instantly inundated by a wave of little boys.

"Hey!" she protested as she bounced off the third step. The wave went by her—five little boys, each one taller than the next. And then a high pleasant voice behind her, apologizing.

"I'm Carrie Wilson," the tall thin woman said, offering a hand up.

"That—crowd...they're all yours?" Maeve managed a smile as she brushed herself down and completed the introduction.

"All mine," Carrie mourned. "For my sins. Oh, that's not true. I love each and every one of them—when I can remember their names. You must be our new neighbor."

"Just moved in," Maeve admitted. "There seem to be a number of empty houses in the area."

Carrie Wilson stepped closer and dropped her voice. "That's because people are moving out, not in," she said confidentially. "I see you're with Ash Corbet. Good man that, if he only had a real job. Met Rob Stanley yet?"

"We—met accidentally," Maeve stammered, unwilling to commit herself further.

"Nothing Stanley does is accidental," Carrie told her. "He's out to buy up all the settlement. I guess he must be pretty near to closing the deal because he was around all last week looking us over."

"Why in the world would he want all this?" Maeve waved vaguely at the dreary scene that surrounded them.

"Bobby!" Carrie screamed. "Stop beating on your brother!" She ran a nervous hand through her black mane of hair, and re-tied the thong that held it in a ponytail. "I don't think anyone knows," she confided again. "But, you know, there's talk about smuggling, like it was in the old days."

"Good Lord," Maeve commented. "Smuggling?"

"It used to be alcohol, during Prohibition," Carrie continued hurriedly. "Now it could be most anything! We're getting out of here ourselves as soon as we can find a house down at Cedar Creek." The boys up ahead of her were coagulating into a gang fight. "I do have to run. Be careful what you do with Stanley. And come and see us when you can. We're at number sixteen, over there. Got to run!" And indeed she did, high heels and all, up the stairs like a cross-country Olympian. In a moment the fight was under control, and Ash Corbet was back at her side.

"So you've met the Wilsons," he said. "Wonderful bunch. He's a writer—some sort of novels, I believe." He was patting her head again, and she resented it, but hardly knew what to do. "I've settled your problem with the telephone company. Since the instrument is already in the house, all they have to do is turn things on at the switching center."

"Why, that's very kind of you," she murmured. "How can I repay you?"

"Very easily." The hand had moved from her head to her shoulder. She shifted her weight uneasily. "I have to get to work today. But how about if we go riding tomorrow? I'll show you around, introduce you to my friends. Things like that. About nine o'clock?"

There were too many little pieces of bait, but Maeve just couldn't decide which to bite on. Meet my friends? Is he serious about that? Work? Riding? Riding what? So she took a deep breath and jumped in over her head.

"Work? I didn't know lawyers worked."

"How sharper than a serpent's tongue," he said wistfully.

"Get it right," she corrected him. "That deals only with children."

"And an intellect to boot?" he asked. She could feel the little touch of sarcasm, and once again felt the impulse to hit him. But he wasn't getting any smaller, standing there. "It's June," he continued. "Vacation time. Nevertheless I feel obliged to put in a couple of days a week at the office."

"I suppose you're going to sue me, too?"

"Sue you?"

"You'll think of a reason. I've bought the entire settlement." She had meant to say something else, but bit her tongue into silence as she anxiously watched the expression on his face. It changed not a whit. Still the studied pleasant man, he was—or the best actor this side of the Florida Keys!

"Why, I don't think I will," he said. "I think between the two of us we can work out a solution to your problem. Besides, you told me you were being sued by a multitude, and I'm the kind of man who hates to wait in line."

Time to change the subject, Maeve told herself. Thin men think too much. Isn't that what Shakespeare said? "Mr. Stanley——" she started out, and then hesitated. "He came to see me—he wants to tear down my sea wall. Why would he want to do that? He *knows* it's on my property. But—why would he want to tear down my wall? Just to show his importance in the community?"

"It's not that sort of wall." He was sporting a broad grin now, as if she had said something funny—or stupid. And Maeve McCormac didn't care for either application. She could see the little gears clicking behind his soft brown eyes. I've told him too much! Maeve screamed at herself.

"Then perhaps you could explain it to me," she said. "In small words." Even he might have noticed how chilly things had become.

"I'd do better to show you," he decided. "Come on." His hand was under her elbow, leading her across to the driveway before she'd even made up her mind. Beowulf, confused, tagged along behind. By the time they had reached his Cherokee four-wheel drive, Maeve was fuming. He had to let go of her arm to open the car door. She shrugged herself away from him.

"I don't go with men unless *I* decide to go," she announced so very precisely that he noticed. Standing as she was with her legs slightly apart, hands on hips, auburn hair gleaming in the Florida sun, teeth half bared, Maeve McCormac looked like a small bomb about to explode.

"Ah, I've done it again, haven't I?" he said. "My mother keeps telling me that I'm too impetuous. Ima——"

"Ma—Mary," she interrupted, shaking with fury.

"I don't know how I passed the Bar exams with such a terrible memory," he sighed. "Mary, I beg your pardon. Would you consider driving with me down to the beach so I can show you what's wrong with the wall?"

It was like a bucket of cold water dumped over her head, that gentle apology from such a big man. It extinguished her fires immediately.

"I—don't mind." The words were barely out of her mouth before she was ushered somewhat forcefully into the front seat. And before she could even muster a "hey there!" he had coaxed Beowulf into the back seat and come around to the driver's side. She shook her head. There seemed to be only an "on" or "off" switch to this man. Either he didn't go at all, or he went triple a normal person's speed. It wasn't many times that this daughter of Irish kings found herself short of words, but this was one of them. She brushed down her dress, shrugged again, and leaned back to see what was going to happen.

He took the short dirt street from the general store directly to the beach, and then used the beach itself as a road, his tires biting into the softer sand as if it were snow. It had taken Maeve twenty minutes to walk up to the store; they came back in five.

"Now, come take a look," he challenged as he vaulted out of the car and then waited impatiently for her to do likewise. He shed his shoes and socks at the water's edge and plunged out into the Cove, paying no attention to the fact that his trouser legs were getting soaked. Maeve paused for a second, and then followed suit. Beowulf, not exactly an aquatic dog, stayed on the beach, whining and dashing back and forth in his concerns. After she'd waded out for about fifteen feet the water was still not up to her knees. He stopped there and led her over to the wall.

"Forty years ago," he told her, "about the time this sea wall was built, you could sail a boat up to that wharf and find a fathom of water under her keel. Since then the wall has forced the waves to drop sand, which has gradually silted up the entire area. Give it a few more years and you won't be able to float a sail board in the area. We need to take the wall out, and let the natural ocean currents and tides scour the harbor."

"And that's what it's about?"

"Well, if it were *my* land, that's exactly what I'd do," he assured her. "What do you think?"

"I don't know, do I?" she answered, nibbling at her lower lip again. "How can I be sure that it's all that simple?"

"I take it you don't know a great deal about sailing?"

"You could say that," she agreed cautiously. "Why would I want to improve the sailing conditions in these parts?"

"To make this a more popular place? To increase your land values?"

To make the area a better target for a development scheme? she asked herself as she watched his facile face. "I'd have to think it over," she concluded and started wading back toward the beach.

"Yes, of course," he said coolly, and she could see all the enthusiasm squeezing itself out of his pores and falling away into the green-tinted water of the Gulf. Back on dry ground, she watched him with a helpless feeling in her mind as he gave her the slightest of nods and scrambled back into his Cherokee. She was still watching as he zoomed around the curving bulk of Watch Hill and disappeared from sight.

"I don't know what I'm doing," she told Beowulf as the great dog came up beside her and sat down. "Why would I want to make the channel out here deeper?" Beowulf whined about his own lack of knowledge. "The question really is, why does Mr. Stanley want to make the channel deeper?" She dropped to the sand, smoothing her skirts beneath her as she fell into the yoga position, already deep in thought. Why?

Smuggling! It came to her suddenly, out of the blue. What Carrie Wilson had said back at the general store... The rumors were going around about using the Cove for smuggling! Smugglers Cove! You have the name, now you'll have the game! And the fact that Stanley looks so open and honest and interesting doesn't have anything to say about what he *might* do. Of course, he would have no need to sue her over the rest of the property. He was only interested in the wharf, and a deep-water channel alongside it!

It was a very confused, discouraged Maeve McCormac who trudged back up the beach, her dog hanging his head behind her as if he bore the same heavy weight. So she spent the rest of the day cleaning the house. It needed it.

Beowulf woke her up just after sunrise the next morning, sniffing around her feet, looking for his breakfast. It had been really her first night in the house. On the previous night she had slept over in the motor home. Last night, after a marathon cleaning session, she had made her bed up in the house itself. And now Beowulf, who was unaccustomed to living in a real house, was making trouble. "Monster!" she groaned at him, not being a morning person at all. He sat down on the rug next to the bed and begged. On a smaller dog it might have looked appealing; with Beowulf's size and shape he looked more like a teaser in a movie called *Monster Munches Munich!* Or some such.

Maeve swung her feet out of bed reluctantly, managed to find her way to the bathroom with one eye open, and finally landed up in the kitchen, dressed in a tired pair of blue jeans, a well-laundered blue blouse that once might have been cerulean, and a worn pair of carpet slippers. Her sparkling auburn hair ran wild in a confusion of curls, but she had, by now, pried both green eyes open.

Beowulf had already wolfed down his breakfast, and was gnawing at the dish impatiently when the telephone rang. The startlingly shrill sound in the once-quiet house shook them both. The dog abandoned his dish and ran for the living room, where the instrument sat in solitary dignity in the middle of the floor. Maeve was close behind him.

He barked once at the ringing instrument, brushed at it with one swipe of his massive paw, and growled into the receiver. Maeve managed to rescue the offending machine. Her dog hated modern technology.

"Hello," her wheelchair-bound mother said in her ear. "Tell that monstrous dog of yours I wish him the same!"

"Mom," Maeve gasped. "I just got up. How did you get this number?"

"No problem at all," her mother responded. "I managed to get a real person at the phone company instead of a computer. I asked for the number at number sixty-two, Smugglers Cove, and there you are!"

"Don't knock the computers," Maeve said dryly. "They still support us."

"Maybe," Mrs. McCormac returned, "but I want grandchildren, not electrons."

"Well——" Maeve stalled, trying to think of some new answer to an old dilemma. "It takes two, Mom," she sighed. "All the good ones seem to be already taken."

"So buy yourself a nice dress, get your hair done, and don't act so darned smart," her mother advised. There was an intimate little laugh behind the stern words—a laugh that bespoke years and oceans of love. "And I've had four calls from Admiralty Shoes, love. They desperately want you to call them back. The number is——"

"I know what the number is," Maeve assured her. "Don't worry about it. Desperate, were they?"

"Desperate," her mother assured her. "There was something about agreeing to all your terms, willing to ship the money in old shoe boxes—whatever. Yes, I'd say they were desperate. Now——"

"Hello, the house!" Some fool male voice, deep-timbred, sounded out in the kitchen. Beowulf dashed for the door and let out a disgustingly friendly whine.

"Guard dog! Hah!" Maeve muttered into the telephone. "Hold on a minute, Mom. There's some sort of local infestation in my kitchen." Mrs. McCormac, long accustomed to her daughter's moods, chuckled and waited. Maeve slammed the phone down, had second thoughts, picked up the instrument and muttered, "Sorry about that," and placed it gently on the cushion next to her. So when she walked out into the kitchen she was already angry.

Beowulf was sitting in the center of the kitchen floor, wagging his tail madly and looking over his shoulder uncertainly at his approaching mistress. "And you'd damn well better worry," she snorted at the animal. "Guard dog! Hah!"

"You said that once already," he commented.

"And just what the h—devil are you doing in my house, Mr. Herbet?" she demanded. Both her hands rode her rounded hips, and sparks tracked from her eyes.

Good Lord, he thought, the higher she flares the more beautiful she looks. Even with her hair dressed as tastefully as a mop! How would you like to take that one home to bed with you, Ash?

"Well, Mr. Sherbet?"

"Corbet," he insisted. "Ash Corbet. We were going——"

"Oh, my Gawd," she grumbled as she interrupted him. "I haven't even had breakfast yet."

"Neither have I," he chuckled. "Breakfast getting is hard on a bachelor. Why don't you whip up something tasty for the both of us?"

"I'll whip you..." she muttered, searching the corners of the room for a broom.

"Uh-uh-uh, naughty," he warned, shaking an index finger at her. "You *did* promise—is someone still on the phone?"

"My mother," she gasped. "And—long distance at that! What are you *doing*?"

"Start fixing breakfast," he ordered as he brushed by her into the living room and picked up the telephone. The shock was too much for her. Her blood began to boil. Rage wrinkled the corners of her eyes as her face turned red. By that time he was back again, almost as quickly as he had gone.

"Your mother says I would risk my life trying to eat your cooking," he said as he walked by her again. "So I'll make the breakfast; you go talk to her!"

Maeve rushed for the telephone. "Mother!" she growled. Indignation filled the wires, and probably spilled over into other more normal conversations on the same cable.

"He sounds very nice," her mother returned placidly. "Very nice. How does he look?"

Too honest to lie, Maeve sighed. "Very nice," she mumbled, hoping Ash wouldn't overhear. "Did you get those payments?"

"Change of subject?" Her mother laughed delightedly. "Meaning it's none of my business—butt out? Or is he listening?"

"Exactly," her daughter said grimly. "Those payments?"

"Everything's working out just as you explained," Mrs. McCormac said. "I had forgotten what cash looked like. It's pretty strange having the mailman delivering boxes of money, love. I'm very lucky, having such a clever daughter."

"Now, Mom!"

"I know," her mother chortled. "He's looking and you're blushing! Well, that's enough small talk. Now tell me why you're down there in that swamp."

"It's not exactly a swamp—not right here." Maeve's mind meandered, using small talk as a defense while she thought. "The swamp is all around us, but we have perhaps ten square miles of high land here—except, they tell me, when the Suwannee River overflows. So the swamp is to the back of us, and north of us, then there's a wildlife preserve—mostly swamp—and then there's us in this spot of high ground.''

"I'm sure that's nice," her mother agreed. "Stop evading the question. Why are you there?"

"Mother, I—he's just in the next room. It has to do with Uncle Shamus. He's been here. I've *got* to find him before I go out of my mind!"

"Oh, Lord, that man again. I've told you and told you, Maeve, he's no relative of ours. Is this man you've accumulated——"

"Mother!"

"So, perhaps I mis-phrased it. Is this man an accomplice?"

"Not exactly." Maeve tried to lean forward into the telephone, to speak more softly. "He's a strange one. An unemployed lawyer or something. And, yes, I'm dead in Florida, too. I can't talk any more. That man's in my kitchen!"

"Better him than you," her mother chuckled, and then hung up. Maeve set the receiver carefully back on its rack, shaking her head. If only children could pick their own parents, she thought laughingly, I'd—I'd choose the one I've got over anybody in the world!

Ash was pouring coffee into two unmatched mugs when she stomped back into the kitchen. A mound of scrambled eggs centered the platter, with a row of toast marching around the foothills—already buttered toast! A few sausages stood triumphantly atop Egg Mountain.

Maeve slid cautiously into her chair. Beowulf was instantly beside her, his muzzle cupped in her free hand. "Go ahead, sample," Ash Corbet encouraged. "Your mother sounds like a fine lady."

She used her fork to steal the tiniest sample of the eggs. They tasted magnificent! It was an effort to slow her hand from "grab" to "polite," as she shoveled eggs onto her plate, decimated the toast, and stabbed two of the four sausages with her fork.

"Yes, my mother is a fine lady," she affirmed, and then plunged back into the affray. Twenty minutes later, comfortably stuffed, she shoved the plate away, pulled the coffee mug over in front of her, nibbled on the last crust, and looked him over.

"You'd make some girl a wonderful husband," she told him. "Do you bake and sew as well?"

"No, not hardly." His grin spread from ear to ear. "I buy all my baked goods, and when something needs sewing I get rid of it."

"Ah, for the life of the idle rich," Maeve drawled. "I can sew. Are there any more at home like you?"

"Not a one." He leaned both elbows on the table and stared at her. "An only lonely child. Don't you feel a little sympathy toward me?"

Maeve pushed her chair back from the table. "Not a bit," she maintained firmly. "Now, what was it that brought you here?"

"There is one important thing——" He improvised a leer.

"That's disgusting!" she snapped. "I meant—like—something to be done outdoors."

"This can be done outdoors," he insisted. His grin expanded as her temper climbed. He's doing this all on purpose, she told herself, but knowing it was so didn't necessarily mean *she* could control her temper.

"I said that's disgusting!" she shouted at him. He pushed his chair back from the table and stood.

"Disgusting?" he queried. "My, you have a short temper, Mae."

"Don't call me that!" she roared at him. Beowulf whined anxiously and dived under the table.

"Your mother told me I should," he said. "I never have heard of horseback riding referred to as disgusting. Are you sure you've got the right trade?"

Horses? Maeve clenched both hands tightly, digging the nails into the tender palms as she struggled to come down off her rage. It took some time. And only then did she count to ten and back, and then glance out of the window. Horses. Plural. Both tied to her battered back fence.

"You did that on purpose, didn't you?" she muttered defensively.

"Bring the horses?" His question was all innocence. "Of course. I said I would. I always keep my promises. Scout's honor, and like that."

And you need to keep on his good side—if he has one—Maeve told herself fiercely. If he recalls Uncle Shamus to the police I won't have a leg to stand on. She remembered that incident down in Texas. The police had arrested her on a fraud charge, her local lawyer had pleaded double jeopardy because she was already dead, the local judge had agreed, and then sentenced her to fifteen days under a Jane Doe warrant! And all because of Uncle Shamus!

"I'm sorry," she said stiffly. "I beg your pardon. Shall we go?"

He looked at her suspiciously. He knew of nothing more dangerous than a quiet volcano. And then he modified the thought. A quiet tiny redheaded volcano. Walk softly, Ash Corbet.

"It would probably be better if you put on shoes, or boots—if you have them," he suggested. "And something to cover your head? The sun is pretty hard to deal with in these parts. And a bathing suit?''

They rode for about half an hour across the length and breadth of the little community. Or, more correctly, Ash did. Once she'd been boosted into the saddle and given some basic instruction, Maeve found that the lovely white mare had a vocabulary of her own, in which the word "Go" just didn't appear. Eventually, with Ash leading her animal by the reins as Maeve clung desperately to the horn of the western saddle, they managed to edge down to the beach, where the procession came to a halt.

"And how was that?" he asked jovially as he swung her from the saddle.

"I'm not sure," she returned, rubbing her foundation. "I haven't been on a horse since I was six years old——''

"Ten years ago?"

She hated that arrogant smile, but the wording was attractive. So attractive that she felt the need to rebut the thought before he got any other wild ideas. "Twenty years ago," she corrected primly. "That *is* what you wanted to know, isn't it? How old I am?"

"I do believe you've got me," he chuckled. "But you'll never get me to believe you're twenty-six. Never."

"I don't mind," Maeve told him. "Believe what you want." She took a couple of steps to test her muscles, and looked around, inspecting her own segment of beach. Beowulf was running back and forth, challenging the waves, trying to catch a floating stick like some puppy. Blue sky above made green water in the shallows below, and directly in front of her was the rickety old wharf she had seen before. The only wharf in this segment of the Cove, apparently.

Without thinking, she asked, "Doesn't anyone around here have a pier except me?"

"Looks as if," he said, laughing. "Can't be a smuggler without a pier."

"That pier——" She gestured back with her head. "It could handle pretty big boats?"

"If it didn't fall down," he agreed. "There's about five or six feet of water at its far end at high tide. Come a moon tide, you could get most any kind of a boat up there. Thinking of doing a little bootlegging?"

"Well, I don't know, do I?" And your mouth is going to get you in big trouble one of these days, she reminded herself. She turned around sharply to look at him. He was calmly unzipping his trousers. She wheeled back in the other direction as fast as her feet would move. "What——?" she stuttered. "What are you doing?"

"Going swimming," he answered. "I *do* have a bathing suit on under all this, Little Miss Modesty." A quick peek from the corner of her eye confirmed his statement, and that disturbed her more than anything else.

"I'm *not* a prude," she said. "I just—you surprised me."

"Of course. Are you coming in?"

"In a minute."

He shrugged his shoulders and trotted out into the water, Beowulf pacing along beside him. He seemed to go an endless distance before the water reached his waist. He turned to wave at her, and then dived cleanly under the water and was gone. The dog, beyond his depth for once, executed a quick turn and a neat dog paddle, heading back to shore. And, with that, Maeve started at her own buttons and zips, lecturing herself all the while about sophistication and growing up. When everything else had fallen away, she stood revealed in her beige bikini. At a distance, the color of the suit matched her light tan, and made it look as if she were wearing nothing at all.

The Gulf water was warm, here in the shallows. Maeve trotted out eagerly until she reached the steep falloff that led to deep water. Ash had stopped at the same point, with the water at waist level; Maeve balanced precariously, with the level just above her breasts. Beowulf was chasing a water crab at the edge of the sand; Ash's head was barely visible, a long way out. Maeve took a deep breath and dived in.

She swam as she did almost everything, with quiet efficiency and grace, ghosting through the water for a few feet in an Australian crawl, then rolling over on her back in a gentle backstroke. Gulls squalled overhead. Beowulf splashed in the shallows. Little wavelets rippled in her ear. Peaceful.

Until a body surged up from underneath her, and the silence was broken by a splash, a roar, and a "Gotcha!"

She rolled away and spurted for the very end of the pier, close at hand. She raced, until a large hand closed around her small ankle, and she was drawn back into his arms.

"Damn!" he exclaimed. "I've been entirely misled!" She struggled against his strong arms and then gave up and let her body land on him. He trod water in one place, and her additional weight was too much. Gradually they sank, nose to nose, down to the bottom, where they were some three feet under the surface. He kicked off the bottom and they shot to the surface. His lips aimed for her mouth, but her evasion tactics won her a buss on the cheek. They began to sink again.

Maeve blew outward to clear her nose, and shook her head. Her crown of curls scattered drops of water in every direction. She offered her right hand for his inspection. The nails were slender and red and sharp.

"Turn me loose," she threatened, "or I'm going to rearrange your pretty face."

He gave her a little push. She floated gently up against one of the pilings of the wharf. "So you finally noticed," he teased.

She was not fool enough to bite on something like that.

"Well," he drawled, "from a distance I thought you hadn't brought a suit to wear." It was a lame comment. She offered it the sniff of derision that it deserved. "Say, you're one tough lady," he sighed. "Okay, I give up. I apologize. Abjectly. I'll bow down and kiss your foot if you insist, but——"

It was too much for her sense of humor to ignore. All the lovely words lined up in a row, and a hang-dog expression on his face to boot. And there's no doubt about it, she thought—he is pretty! "Don't be a fool," she giggled as she cast off from the piling and headed for shore at flank speed. He was a good swimmer himself. Even with his late start, they both ran aground at the same time, scrambled to their feet, and raced ashore.

Somehow, in those last ten seconds he was ahead of her, and waiting as she staggered to a stop, her eyes half blinded by the salt water, panting for breath. She ran squarely into him, bounced, and was gathered back up again.

It was almost as if a cloud had come across the sun. In one second they were both laughing, gasping for breath. In the next they stood hard up against each other, separated only by a few wisps of cloth. The air was heavy with tension.

One of her hands was trapped at his waist. The other came up to brush the hair out of her eyes. She peered up at him, vaguely wondering at her own feelings. She looked up at his broad craggy pixie face and the line of freckles that marched across his nose, and felt the soft proud contact as her breasts flattened against him. It was too much to resist, and she was in no mood for resisting in any case.

He shifted one arm up to her shoulders and turned her slightly until she was off balance, resting her entire weight on his arms. Her lips twitched nervously. Her green eyes blinked twice, then shut tight of their own volition. She had meant only to let him touch and tease her lightly, but when his lips made contact something seemed to go wrong. There was more man in this tall thin frame than she had ever anticipated. Something banged against her spine, and a wild spiral of fire stirred all her sexual reactions.

She might perhaps have let him move on to phase two, but it suddenly came to her attention that the banging on her spine was not a sex impulse, but the butting of a dog. A dog who was not quite sure what was going on, but was working up to a stronger objection in jig time!

"All right, all right," she grumbled, straightening up to glare at Beowulf. "Look. I'm practically brand-new. Not a scratch on me. He didn't even get to the ravishing part!" And why the devil did I say anything like that? she asked herself, puzzled. Her dog backed away and circled to his side of the melee, teeth showing in a very suggestive manner, and by that time Maeve had recovered her senses and squirmed away.

"Now see what you've done," Ash complained mournfully to the dog. "She's got away!"

"Lucky for you, she has," Maeve told him firmly as she grabbed up her beach towel. "The next time I go out with you, Octopus, I'm going to program my dog to eat first and complain later!"

"That's the trouble with women these days," Ash continued, as if she hadn't said a word. "No spunk. Well, come on. My friends are waiting to meet you."

"Not today," Maeve muttered. "For some strange reason I think I've seen enough of the Sherbet family for one day."

"So, tomorrow," he offered. "And I'd hate to change my family name. Corbet. Say it after me—Corbet."

She glared at him, then spun on her heel and headed for home. Beowulf followed, but reluctantly. As she slammed her kitchen door behind them, she muttered, "Why in God's name did I let him do that? What in the world is going on in my stupid little mind?"

Beowulf barked, lending a sharp exclamation point to the whole exercise.

CHAPTER THREE

MAEVE got up from a crumpled bed just at sunrise. Her eyes were half closed, her mind as crumpled as her bed. Three faces had circled in her head all night long. Rob Stanley—definitely the bad guy? Or just a developer who had met his match in her Uncle Shamus? Packy Schultz—eight decades on the wrong side of the law, so why should he change now? And Ash Corbet, the enigma. Unofficial mayor of a tumbledown settlement; lawyer with nowhere to practice; painter with no enthusiasm for his own work? Something was definitely rotten in Denmark.

"And you're no better than the rest of them," she muttered as her feet hit the floor. "Liar, forger—and, dear God, what else before I get through? But I need the money!" Beowulf, who slept beside her bed whether she was in it or not, muttered dog complaints, shifted his huge weight, and went back to sleep. "Admiralty Shoes," Maeve told herself. "That's where the money is." She snatched up her bedraggled linen robe and shuffled out into the van.

Before going to bed the night before, she had moved the telephone out of the house into her work compartment in the van. Now she plugged the receiver into her computer modem, and quickly dialed the number of the shoe company. Her machine reached their machine, identities were established, and presently her printer was spewing out yards of paper. Three hours later she scratched her head and chortled. Computer programs delighted her more than detective stories, whether they were honest or otherwise. And this one was otherwise. She crowed in delight as she circled the hardly noticed segment of instructions with her red pencil.

"Neat," she told herself in admiration. "Why steal a lot and get everyone's attention when you can steal a little bit every day, unnoticed?" And at that point her nose twitched. Someone was cooking bacon—*in her house!*

Living alone taught a woman many small cautions. Not guns; Maeve abhorred guns. Her baseball bat lounged by the van door. She picked it up and hefted it, slipped out of her slippers, and tiptoed back into the house. Beowulf was missing from the bedroom. A bad sign? Someone was in the kitchen, humming away. Her guardian dog was sitting halfway across the kitchen threshold, managing to wag his tail enthusiastically. Maeve shifted the bat into both hands, took a deep breath, and vaulted over her dog to land next to the kitchen table.

"Don't make a move," she yelled, "or I'll—— Oh, it's you again!" Disgusted, she lowered the bat, and barely missed her own toes.

"Me indeed." Ash Corbet stood at the stove, dressed in shorts but no top, the whole enveloped in one of her long butcher's aprons. It wasn't all that long on him. In fact, his bare legs projected well below the hem. Muscular legs. Long, no-nonsense legs, heavily tanned.

"Yes, I remember that your mother said you could hardly boil water, so I thought I'd drop in and make you an edible breakfast. I didn't expect such a gracious welcome, though. Bacon and eggs all right?" He turned in her direction. Suddenly he looked like a virile male wearing nothing but an ornate apron, and for some strange reason Maeve found herself licking her dry lips.

"Bacon and eggs?" he prompted. "It'll do you a world of good. Put hair on your—well, that's not necessary, is it? It'll wake you up in a good temper so we can spend the day together."

"I *always* eat cornflakes," she growled at him. "And I *never* get up with a bad temper. Furthermore, today is a working day."

"And you're not sure you'd go about with me even if you couldn't find an excuse?" Laughter was teasing the corner of his mouth, and sparkled from his deep dark eyes. Standing still and glaring was tiresome work. Maeve fought off her own smile for just a second, and then gave up.

"You frightened me," she complained. "I hate people who sneak up on me... What the devil are you doing now?"

He had reached into the back pocket of his shorts and pulled out a little notebook. "No sneaking up," he muttered as he printed something in the book. He made an effort of the writing, his stub of a pencil barely visible in his big hand, the tip of his tongue protruding from the side of his mouth. "There. I have a lousy memory. Always write everything down—that's what my mother taught me."

Maeve's eyes were glued to his face, and missed the facile movement that transferred the notebook back to his pocket. It might have been a warning about this complex man, but she failed to note it. "That—must be a nice habit," she said, sighing. "I——"

"Don't believe it," he replied with a chuckle. "I keep losing the notebooks. Now, milady Mae, sit thee down."

Like any good little girl, hypnotized by those eyes, she did as she was told.

The bacon was not quite as well-cooked as she liked. The eggs were beyond compare. Beowulf, who had expected to participate, grumbled a protest. The two humans ate away, paying him no attention at all.

"Good," Maeve finally pronounced, her mouth still clogged with toast. And then a moment later, after sipping from her cup, "But is this coffee?"

"Yes, it's coffee. I think the taste has something to do with swamp water leaking into our well—*your* well, pardon me." He set his half-filled plate down on the floor, and Beowulf promptly deserted his mistress. "Now, then, Miss—Kennedy?"

Maeve choked on the last of the coffee before she remembered who she was. "Yes. Mary Kennedy. Born and raised in Fulton County, Georgia. Why are *you* interested?"

He grinned at her as his eyes measured her figure.

"Business interest," she said firmly.

"Ah. That. Well, I am all the law there is in Smugglers Cove, Miss Mary Kennedy. Naturally I'm interested in every newcomer to the area. What, for example, do you do for a living—besides look glamorous?"

"You need your eyes examined," Maeve snapped at him. She tapped her forefinger on the table for a moment, then got up and went to fetch her wallet. Where once it had been almost empty, now it bulged with little cards and pictures. Packy Schultz owned a small letterpress, and had spent the previous evening running off all manner of things for her.

"Try this," she said as she came back, and flipped a business card in front of him. It carried a fancy logo, her assumed name in beautiful script, and under it in bold print, "Computer Consultant."

"And a picture of my mother at home." Dropped in front of him, on top of her calling card. "And my last month's telephone bill," purportedly from Southern Bell, but actually another product of Packy's fertile mind. "And my membership card to the Daughters of the Confederacy. Does that satisfy your curiosity, Sheriff?"

"Well—Deputy, actually. It's a big county, you know. Daughter of the Confederacy, huh?"

"Among other things. Now, perhaps you have something that will identify *you*?"

His face turned red. His shorts fitted him like a glove; there was obviously not enough space available for anything but him and his notebook inside them. "You've got me there," he replied. "Don't happen to have a thing with me. I even left my badge at home. But surely my making your breakfast reassures you?"

"You bet." She glared at him across the table. "Al Capone was noted for his pasta, too."

"Low blow," he muttered.

Maeve's glare broke up into little pieces as she giggled. She might have said something else, but was interrupted.

"Hello, the house!" A loud deep voice from outside. Beowulf snapped to attention and growled as he moved to the door, his busy nose working the cracks at the threshold.

"Mr. Stanley," Maeve guessed. She pushed her chair back and started across the room.

"Oh, Gawd," Ash Corbet grumbled. He snatched at his plate and utensils, stuffed them into the sink, and made for the living room at high speed.

"You and he are not friends?" Maeve paused, one hand on the doorknob, and watched Corbet. The little grin on her face turned the innocuous question into some sort of insinuation which he failed to appreciate.

"Not precisely," Ash admitted. "If you don't mind, I'll just keep out of sight for a time."

Maeve shrugged her shoulders as he faded from sight. She was somewhat nervous, herself. She rubbed both palms on her robe, latched on to Beowulf's collar, and managed to get the door open. Big blond Rob Stanley was leaning negligently against the post of the back porch, a mile-wide smile on his face. Maeve cautiously pushed the screen door half open and peered around him. The man was all alone.

"No lawyers?" she inquired. Beowulf growled, not exactly welcoming. Maeve shook the dog's collar gently.

"That was a foolish thing for me to say," Stanley said apologetically. "I was just a trifle—upset. It had been a hard day. The work, you understand, and that—that McCormac man. And then my mother isn't feeling too well, you know. I thought perhaps we might start all over again, Miss—why, I don't even know your name."

No, you surely don't, Maeve told herself, and when we finish this day you still won't know! And in the meantime...

"Do come in, Mr. Stanley. I recognize what a disturbing week you must be having. I'm Mary Kennedy." Her little hand was swallowed up; Beowulf grumbled a couple of times, but stood aside.

"Rob," the big man insisted. "Never could get accustomed to that Mr. Stanley business. Mary Kennedy, eh? Love that name—Mary. And pretty as a picture, too."

And that makes *two* blind men in one morning, Maeve told herself. Or two practiced liars! She gestured toward a chair, and set the kettle boiling. "Instant coffee?"

"Don't mind if I do." He dropped into one of the elderly kitchen chairs, which creaked a protest but held on. Rob Stanley. Wearing a cowboy shirt, a gray and blue kerchief tied at his bull neck, a pair of faded jeans, and doffing a dusty cream Stetson. And boots with three-inch heels. He fumbled with his hat until Maeve rescued it. There was an old hat rack by the back door. She hung the Stetson decorously and turned back to the whistling kettle.

He made small talk about the weather until she placed a steaming mug in front of him, and brought milk and sugar—which he ignored. "Yes, sir, made a real ass of myself the other day," he announced. "The surprise, I guess. Say you bought all this property?"

"Lock, stock, and——" pier, she was about to add, but decided against it. The pier might be a sensitive subject "—beach," she substituted. "It seemed like a bargain, and I had considerable cash on hand, so——"

"Investments," he said, shaking his head. "Best thing for a girl your age to be doing. Put your money into investments. Land. Can't beat it. God isn't making any more of it. Value's bound to go up." He sipped at his cup, managing to hide his distaste. Maeve struggled to hide her smile. Even with instant coffee she was an instant failure.

"Nice coffee! I don't suppose you'd be willing to let me see that bill of sale again?" he proposed. He can't see, and he can't taste. Maeve recorded it in her spacious mind. What else can't he do?

"No, I wouldn't mind. It's only a copy, of course. The original is stored in my lawyer's safe. Just a second."

She pushed her chair back and went out into the van. Ash Corbet was standing just behind the door, a shushing finger to his lips. Maeve struggled to keep from sticking her tongue out at him, and quickly found the document Stanley wanted to see.

"Ah. Filed and registered in Gatesville, Coryell County, Texas," the big man said.

"Oh, is it?" She had to bite her tongue to hold back any more comments. Her forged bill of sale had been considerably embellished since she last scanned it. Packy Schultz might be an eighty-year-old ex-con, but he possessed as fertile a mind as any partner might need. The seal of the Registrar of Deeds fairly sparkled at her— also forged. "Yes. I had forgotten."

He was reading the document more carefully, for the third time, ignoring his coffee. It almost seemed that he was memorizing the entire thing. But then finally he set it aside. "You could make a quick profit," he said, sighing. "I'll pay you ten percent more than you paid for the original purchase."

"I—don't think I could do that," Maeve murmured. "I need a quiet settled place for the next few months— my business requirements, you understand." One more calling card from Packy's horde was slipped in front of his eyes. "Consulting work requires a great deal of quiet. It's a thoughtful task. And Smugglers Cove seems to be just the place."

"Consulting work?"

"Computer systems," she amplified. "Programs. I write them, de-bug them, anything needed. You might say that I'm a computer doctor."

"Lots of other quiet places in Florida," he coaxed. "Fifteen percent above your purchase price?"

"I don't think I could, not just at this time," Maeve said. "I'm in the middle of a big research program. Maybe in a month or so, I might think it over."

"I don't have a——" Stanley snapped, and then recovered himself. "I mean it would be a nice thing to settle it all by the end of the month, but I mustn't hustle the little girl, must I? Well, keep my offer in mind, little lady."

"I'll do that," she said as she stood by the door and handed him his hat. "Do come again."

"Must be a quiet place," he muttered, almost under his breath as he stepped out into the hot Florida sun.

"Yes, you'll be seeing me." Maeve stood at the door until he was out of sight, walking down toward the beach. Before she knew it, Ash Corbet was at her side.

"Don't *do* that," she snapped. "I hate people who——"

"Sneak up on you," he said. "Yes, I remember. Your friend is remarkably interested in a dumpy little settlement, isn't he?"

"He's not *my* friend," Maeve retorted in her chilliest voice. "And Smugglers Cove is *not* a dumpy little settlement. I happen to like it very much. Did you bring a hat?"

"Well, now, a little cool around here, ma'am, isn't it? No, I didn't bring a hat. I own one, but I don't rightly remember where it is."

"Probably among the pile of little notebooks you've lost," she suggested. "Wouldn't this be an ideal time for you to go looking for it? Or them?"

"I do believe I can take a hint," he said, grinning at her. "You'd like me to leave?"

"The very thing. You *are* clever."

"But I'll be back just after lunch," he said cheerily. "We're going fishing, you and I."

"We are?" She hated to see that gleam in his eye as she backed away from him. But no matter how quickly she backed he remained just as close as before. And when she bumped into the wall there was nowhere else to go.

"Don't," she muttered. "Beowulf!" The big dog ignored them both, stretching out on the cool floor on his belly.

So he kissed her. After the first second of contact there hardly seemed to be any reason at all to protest, so she relaxed. Minutes after he'd left Maeve struggled to a chair and sat down hard, her face still red with embarrassment, her breathing still irregular. It was that moment of relaxation, she decided, that had allowed him to do—all that. A girl her age ought to know better. And she certainly would the next time!

Packy Schulz caught up with her the next morning. "Got yourself a good burn," he commented.

"I thought it was cloudy enough to protect me from the sun," Maeve protested. "I'll know better——"

"Next time?" he interrupted.

"There isn't going to *be* any next time," she stated very firmly. "The man's like an octopus!"

"Mr. Stanley?"

"Mr. Corbet," she snapped. "God's gift to the ladies. Or at least *he* thinks so. And to add insult to injury I didn't catch a single fish! Oh, that man!"

The old man chuckled. "Got hisself some reputation, that Ash Corbet. Great talker; lousy painter. Got one of them big country scenes hangin' on his wall, way up near the ceiling over all them machines of his. Get close, an' you can see it's one of them paint-by-the-numbers things. Ain't ashamed to have people know, neither. Laughed like a hyena when I called him on it."

"Machines?" she asked idly as she made him a mug of coffee.

"Like them you got in the van," he said. "Computer things. Enough to put a good penman out of business. Got him all kinds of alphabets and things. Beats my little printing press all to pieces—except he really don't know how to make it all go. Practical, all right, but he's got no imagination. Now—here's the card you really has to have."

"Why—it's a Social Security card," she gasped. "Mary Kennedy! How in the world did you——?"

"Easiest thing in the world," Packy said, chuckling in his high cracked way. "New law says everyone over five years old gotta have one if they're being listed as a tax deduction. So, like the good fellow that I am, I writes the Internal Revenue Service askin' for a card for my daughter, Mary. Naturally, they sends it back almost at once. And there you go!"

"But—but Packy, I'm not five years old!"

"That's the trouble with you young people," he grumbled as he took a sip of coffee. "Don't pay no attention to details. You see your age anywhere on that card?"

Maeve turned it over every which way, and was forced to agree. The card contained a list of printed instructions, her name, her new account number, and a place for her signature. Nothing else. "But if I show it to the Social Security people—— ?"

"Didn't make it to show to them," he snorted. "Made it to show to everybody *but* them. Far as folks can tell, you could be fifty years old if you wanted to. And this afternoon we drives up to Cross City and you shows them your birth certificate and your Social Security card, and you takes the examination for your driver's license. And with all them papers, lady, you are born again!''

"Packy, you're a genius." She rushed around the table and kissed him enthusiastically.

"Probably right," he muttered, but there was laughter in his faded blue eyes. "Now, how about *my* problem?"

"The wine?"

"The wine."

"I don't suppose it could be buried around here someplace?"

"Don't suppose. They wasn't time to bury all that. Had to be hid someplace already prepared. Somewheres in these houses, I think."

"Then all we need to do is search the houses," she replied.

"Oh, sure. All them people, they'll stand at the doors and say, 'Jus' you come right in. The wine's hid in the cellar.' That's what they'll say."

"Ah, but you forget, Packy. I'm the new landlord around these parts. And you're my assistant. Thirty houses? We could inspect six or seven a day, and be finished within the week! You know, make a record of all the repairs needed, find out who's not paying their rent. And, while I'm giving them the sweet-talk, you can be poking in the corners and down the cellars."

Packy's face brightened perceptibly. "Ain't got no cellars anywheres in Smugglers Cove," he commented, "but that's a good idea. I think maybe you missed your callin', little lady. During your off hours I could give you a few lessons."

She blushed, but admitted to herself that *anything* newly learned might be useful.

"Too proud to steal?" the old man teased her.

"I—think it might be nice to have lessons," she answered, "but I'm up to here in work, Packy. What we need is..." She pondered the needs. "We need a leaflet we can deliver to every house, telling them we're coming."

"You write it, I'll print it," he agreed. "Take most of the night..."

"I'll write it, and my computer will print it," she substituted. "Take about twenty-five minutes or so. But you'll have to take copies around to each house tomorrow. Deal?"

"Damned computers," he muttered. "Spoilin' a good trade. But—well, you're the boss, an' the exercise won't hurt." He got up and headed for the door. And isn't that strange? Maeve asked herself. Beowulf hasn't even growled at him!

After the old man had left, she went back to the van and made a long and interesting telephone call to the president of Admiralty Shoes. "A strange program you have," she reported. "Somebody has added a separate set of instructions. On every entry of more than ten thousand dollars your machine is told to round off the extra figures in the hundreds column, and deposit that amount in an account numbered one-two-five-four-eight-six. Whoever he is, the man is stealing almost eight hundred dollars a day from you, every day—four thousand dollars a week. It has to be someone who had something to do with installing your program. Now, about my fee?"

"Lord, I wish we were back in the good old Mafia days," the president muttered. "I could understand the Mafia. Yes, your fee. I don't understand, but—a cheque made out to Mary Kennedy, for services rendered. Yes, I have the new address at Smugglers Cove. Express mail, yes, I understand. And thank you, Maeve. Thank you very much."

Having done her best for the Business World, Maeve McCormac went back to the kitchen and lunched out of a can of chilli con carne.

It was a long drive across the swamp to the county seat. Dixie County was by no means the smallest of all Florida's counties, but if you were to count only *dry* land it might become so. The Suwannee River's source lay up in Georgia, in the Okefenokee Swamp, and as the river wound gently southward it created more swamplands between itself and the Gulf of Mexico. A few daring roads penetrated the swamp in a generally easterly direction, until they joined up with the massive highway ninety-eight. Cross City sat on the highway at the junction of county road three-fifty-one.

"Driven before, Miss Kennedy?" The state trooper was big and uniformed and hot and disinterested.

"About ten years," she answered, unable to hide the little quaver in her voice. "In Mississippi. But I lost my license in a fire some years ago, and never really needed one again until just now. Why do you ask?"

"Because you passed the written test with one hundred per cent," he said, chuckling. "Now, drive me around the block."

It wasn't a difficult drive. Cross City was not exactly loaded with blocks to be driven around. And that was all that was required. The trooper looked casually at her Social Security card, brushed her birth certificate aside, considered her wallet full of family pictures, and issued her with a license.

When he had climbed out of the car and tipped her a salute, Maeve began to breath again. The family pictures were nice, but she had no idea *whose* family they were.

"Told you it would be easy," Packy chortled as he climbed into the car. "Trouble with this world is it has too many honest people in it. Which is lucky, I suppose, or guys like me might have to go to work for a living. Say, ain't that——?"

It was. Ash Corbet, dressed in suit and tie, walking up the steps of the court house, looking as if he owned the place. Packy ducked his head.

"What do you suppose he's up to?" Maeve asked.

"Don't know. Don't wanna know," the old man said as he slid back up in his seat. "Anybody so free with the court house ain't exactly on my callin' list. Let's get back to the Cove and start lookin' at houses."

It was a good idea, but a little impractical. Corbet had popped back out of the court house and hurried across the street to where they were parked.

"Now, isn't this a surprise?" Ash said, his voice booming across the square. "All the way up from the Cove, and two neighbors right here ahead of me. Where's your mutt—I mean dog?"

"Yes. A terrible surprise. My dog is at home, guarding. That's what guard dogs do," Maeve managed to say as she tucked her newly issued license under her thigh, out of sight. "Packy has agreed to help me survey the Cove, you know."

"Yes. I read one of your pamphlets," Corbet returned. "Going all out as a landlord, are you?"

"All the way. What brings *you* to the court house?"

"Nothing special. I told you I was a lawyer, didn't I?"

She nodded her head. Telling and proving are two different things, she told herself.

"So unemployed lawyers tend to hang around the court house," he said. "Actually got me a case—well, I've been assigned as a Public Defender. A man charged with beating his wife. Not much money in it, but an honorable cause."

"I hope he gets fifty years," Maeve said coldly. "Now, if you'll excuse us, we have to get back to work."

She was driving Packy's old Volkswagen. The engine started with a burst of power, and then faltered. Without giving it a thought, angry as she was, she wheeled the vehicle around in an illegal U-turn, right in front of a small group of men including the state trooper, the county sheriff, and the court bailiff. Luckily traffic was light; she zoomed back down highway three-fifty-one with more enthusiasm than good sense.

"Hadn't ought to've done that," Packy advised her as they left the outskirts of town behind them. "Woman workin' on a fake identity has to obey all them little laws. Traffic, and things like that. Don't wanna get anybody curious, ya know. Don't need any investigations. Even a dumb county sheriff could find a loose thread in the weavin'." And Maeve, who knew he was right, shriveled a little in her seat and crossed the fingers on her left hand.

There was no traffic to worry about. She tapped her fingers on the steering wheel as they headed west, her mind on other things. Why is it that Ash Corbet annoys me so much? Any other macho man, and I would have easily ignored him entirely. But one wrong word from Ash Corbet and I'm up in flames. And that doesn't make a lot of sense, because he means nothing to me. Absolutely nothing!

Satisfied that she had nothing to worry about as far as Ash Corbet was concerned, she followed the gradual curve of the highway at a reasonable speed. Dixie County had no intention of pursuing her, evidently, but somebody Up There was watching and meant to get even. No sooner had she come back to the straight stretch of road than the right rear tire blew, the old car began to twist under her hands, and she barely managed to bring it to a halt.

"Damn!"

Packy, who had been dozing off for most of the way, sighed. "You don't know the worst of it. I don't have a tire iron."

"You mean you don't have a spare tire?"

"Oh, I got a spare tire all right, but I don't have no tire iron to change it with."

"Oh, Lord! What do we do now?"

The old man smiled at her. "One thing you learns as you grows older, partner. When in doubt, you waits."

The hot Florida sun beat down on the top of the car, turning the interior into a furnace. For two hours they waited. "Not the most populated road in the state," Packy teased her. "Plenty of water." He gestured to the swamp on either side of the road.

"I can't drink that," Maeve grumbled as she watched the bubbles that formed in the water barely a foot off the roadway. Nervous tension caught up with her. She fumbled in her bag for a cigarette. She had sworn off smoking more than a year ago, but had to have something to do with her hands.

"Don't do the alligators no harm," he chuckled. "Ever seen a river burn?"

"Don't be silly."

"Nothin' silly about it." He watched with his head cocked to one side as she lit up. Like a bird, watching, she thought. One drag on the cigarette filled her lungs with unexpected smoke. She choked, and coughed the rest of it out. Packy whacked her a couple of times on the back.

"Okay, okay," Maeve gasped. Obviously smoking wasn't the answer—was never ever again going to be the answer. Halfway between regrets and pleasure, she flipped the burning butt out into the water.

"Oh, no!" Packy yelled. Maeve raised her eyebrows at him. "You'll burn the damn river!" the old man yelled at her.

"That's just not possible," Maeve replied as she watched the butt arc upward lazily, reach its peak, and fall gently, just as a massive bubble broke the surface of the water. Butt and bubble met. There was a roar like a blowtorch being ignited, and a flash of flame that sputtered at them and then went out.

"I told you," the old man repeated. "Could've burned the whole damn swamp!"

"Try pulling my other leg," she snapped. For the first time since they had met she was not about to humor the man. If he wanted to dream, let him. The bit with the cigarette was a figment—of my imagination? Or a delusion. This is a day for delusions, that's for sure.

"Methane gas," the old man told her. "There's so much debris on the bottom that it decomposes and forms methane. All you gotta do is find the right spot. Sometimes, in high summer, there's so many areas generatin' gas that you can almost set the whole river on fire. Here comes somebody."

"Like a bad penny," Maeve muttered. The car coming up behind them was a two-year-old Chrysler. And the driver was Ash Corbet.

"Have a little trouble, do we?" he asked as he swung his long legs out of the driver's seat. His jacket was missing, as was his tie, but he still looked the well-groomed lawyer.

"No, *we* don't," she snapped, angry now because he looked so cool and collected, while she was dripping perspiration, her neat little dress a mass of wrinkles. "*I* happen to have a flat tire, and no tire iron to fix it with."

"Ah, a little thing like that," he mused, coming over to inspect the damage. Maeve desperately wanted to kick his ankle, and instead kicked the flat tire and injured her toe. Which only made her angrier. It was no *little* thing at all! Packy, who knew a good thing when he saw it, withdrew to the roadside and sat down to watch. Maeve glared at Ash; he smiled gently at her.

"So why don't you——?" he started to say.

"No!"

"You'd prefer me to drive off and leave you here?"

"I—no." Common sense was such an uncommon occurrence that she managed to stifle all her errant feelings and make a poorly worded apology.

"Think nothing of it," he said, and immediately went up ten points in her scoring system by saying, "Why don't you two sit in my car while I change the tire? I've left the air-conditioning on. It'll only take a jiffy."

This particular jiffy was exactly eight minutes and thirty seconds long, and the air-conditioning was wonderful. Marvellous. So when, having finished the repair job, he came over and climbed into his own car, she almost jumped for joy when he added, "Why don't you let Packy drive his car back to the Cove, while you and I follow in mine?"

"I dunno," Packy complained. "I ain't got air-conditionin'."

"Exactly," Ash Corbet said, chuckling. "And that means I get the girl! Mary?"

Hot sun, cool car, young man, old man, blazing sun glaring above her head, quiet in the pool where the methane flame had finally gone out. Carefully Maeve moved over directly in front of the air-conditioner blowers and fluffed her skirts for maximum intake. "I do believe I'll go with Ash," she admitted, and flashed him her most engaging smile.

"If I was fifty years younger you'd never have a chance," Packy muttered at Corbet as he climbed out of the Chrysler and went forward to the old Volkswagen.

CHAPTER FOUR

MAEVE stretched out on the warm sand and sighed with relief. Six days of searching—inventorying—cottages had worn her to the bone. She and Packy Schultz had found no sign of smuggled wine, but six roofs leaked, the community cesspools seemed on the verge of overflow, two families had promptly moved out at the first sound of "rent," and Packy had finally given up. But not before leaving her a clipboard filled with notes in his delightful Spencerian hand.

"I'm just too tired to read it all," she told Beowulf. Her dog panted at her, and did his best to push her off the blanket. Lying on bare sand was something the ancient animal had no intention of doing. If, therefore, his mistress wanted to relax in this oceanic desert, it seemed only proper she should let *him* have the blanket. Or so he mimed.

Maeve smiled at his obvious message, and shifted slightly to one side. She, in her maroon bikini, had even less intention than Beowulf of lying on the roasting-hot sands. But, instead of joining her, the big dog came up on his haunches and growled. Maeve sighed, then turned her head slowly. Towering over her, dressed in a sleek pair of black swimming trunks, wearing flippers and carrying snorkel and mask, was Rob Stanley. His blond hair was plastered back against his head.

"Lovely day." A few drops of water dripped off him and landed on Maeve. "Almost as lovely as you, Mary. I may call you Mary?"

"It's my name," she answered cautiously. "Been swimming?" And if that isn't the non sequitur of the week! she told herself. Been swimming? No, of course not, he's been playing croquet on a lawn where the sprinkler system was turned on! Poor Mr. Stanley. He's probably as honest as the day is long—not like some other men I know—and I keep picking on him. He deserves better! So she gracefully coiled up into a sitting position and gave him a smile.

"Yes." It was the smile that caught him. The two things Maeve needed to turn herself into a raving sex symbol were a bikini and a smile. And, not being the most ignorant lady in the land, she realized it.

"Exploring," he said. "Out at the end of your pier."

Maeve turned around to shade her eyes and look down the rickety length of her dock. "I must try that some time," she mused as she looked back at him, and felt around in her beach bag for her sunglasses. "How's your mother?"

"What? Oh, Mother. Yes, she has her good days and she has her bad days, and this is one of the latter."

"Why, that's too bad." In fact, it touched a little string attached to the corner of Maeve's heart. "Care for the elderly"—one of the tenets of her raising. "Maybe I could come over and keep her company for a time?"

He blanched, and stared at her for a second. "Oh, no," he stammered, "that wouldn't be—my mother doesn't care for company. Especially strangers. We—I try to avoid inviting people to the house. Of course, at the end of the month when she goes back north to my brother's house for the fall season, I'd love to——"

"I just thought to ask," Maeve responded. "I wouldn't dream of imposing on her. So, how's business, Mr.—er—Rob?"

"Well, you know the building trade," he pontificated as he sank to the ground into the space that had been set aside for Beowulf. "Like the elevator business, it has its ups and downs." The look on his face said "that's a joke"; Maeve, who failed to find anything humorous about it, hung on to her determination to be nice to him, and chuckled.

A tension seemed to run out of him as he relaxed. His smile became personable; he looked ten years younger. "No," he continued, "it's hard to find a good plot of land to develop on the Gulf coast. And when I do find a place it's years before it brings in any income. A long-term business, development."

"Yes, I can see that," Maeve said. Her heart really wasn't with the conversation any more. A pair of gulls were dive-bombing the end of her pier in a series of life-or-death flying exercises against a background of gathering storm clouds. So she missed the next sentence or two, and then recognized the silence surrounding them. He was waiting for her to say something.

"I don't know," she hazarded.

"You don't know if you're married?"

"Oh—I misunderstood. Yes, I know that I'm not married. And you?"

"Nor I," he replied. "I always intended to marry young and have four kids, but—but it never seemed to work out. And now I've let it go too long."

"Nonsense, Rob. You're still in good shape, with plenty of good looks and vigor. There's always a time and place for a man like you." Which, she told herself instantly, you've overdone, Maeve McCormac. He acts as if *you're* both the time and the place. "Of course," she added quickly, "I don't know a great deal about it, except for what my fiancé tells me."

Stanley's face dropped a half mile. "Of course," he replied ruefully. "A girl of your charm would be already snapped up. Too bad." He turned away from her to look out to sea. The sun, already far to the west over Texas, was losing the struggle against the oncoming storm. Try another tack, she told herself in reprimand.

"You know, that first day when I came down here and your men were tearing down my wall, I didn't understand."

"Oh? Someone told you about——?"

"About the Cove, and this being the only deep-water spot within twenty miles, and all that. And how my wall was collecting sand and ruining the only pier in the area. It *is* the only pier?"

"The only one," he said somewhat sadly. "I have to anchor my boat offshore around the bend." He waved southward in the general direction of his house and his beach, both out of sight behind Watch Hill. "Dangerous. I wonder?"

She waited for a second, letting the words flutter on the wind. "Wonder what?"

"I wonder if you might be willing to sell me your pier?" he asked hurriedly.

Maeve's clever brain snapped to attention. This was one of the keys to the multiple mysteries of Smugglers Cove. Buy the only pier in the Cove? Well, now, why not play along?

"I—don't think I could *sell* it to you, Rob," she responded. It was hard to prune all the coyness out of her voice. "I have a mother to provide for, too. But I wouldn't be averse to leasing it to you for a short period. Say, a year? I couldn't possibly make it a longer period, not without putting considerable money into it. Repairing the structure, for example. And yes, tearing down the sea wall to let the Gulf scour out a better anchorage."

Rob Stanley startled her. He jumped to his feet, all smiles. Beowulf made a number of discouraging noises, but the property developer had bitten on the hook and could not be deterred. "What a marvellous idea!" he rattled on. "Marvellous, Mary. And, since it's all for my benefit, I would be happy to make the pier improvements, and take down the wall. Shall we say—we'll split the cost?"

"I'd have to have my lawyer look over the contract," she interjected, hating to spoil his parade. "But certainly you could go ahead with removing the sea wall right away."

"Bless your heart, child! I've got to go tell Mother." And with that he kicked off his flippers, gathered them up, and dashed down the beach.

"Good Lord, what sort of man is this?" Maeve muttered. "A little business deal between neighbors, and he has to run and tell his mother?"

She watched the flying figure for a moment, then stood up, shook out her blanket, whistled up her dog, and headed back to the house. It was too confusing. Rob Stanley could hardly be the villain, not if all he wanted was a better anchorage for his boat. Not if he loved his mother all that much! Somewhere in the back of her mind a voice warned, Your Uncle Shamus is a nice guy. Everyone admires him until he steals them blind. I'll bet *he* loves *his* mother too! A few drops of rain spattered her. She increased her lazy walking speed.

Wearily she found her way through the sawgrass, kicked her sandals off on the tiny back porch and went into the house. No sooner had she entered the house when the downpour came. Beowulf, heading immediately for his water dish, splashed away like a runaway waterfall. Maeve wandered into the shower, enjoyed the bliss of cool clear water for a time, wrapped herself in a towel, and headed for the telephone. The "mother" theme had reminded her. She picked up the instrument and dialed home.

It was the busiest telephone line she had ever used. Three times she dialed without result. On the fourth attempt the telephone at the other end rang, and her mother answered. Their conversation was light, family, with a few exceptions. There seemed to be thundercrashes on the line, intermittent interruptions, and, on occasion, two or three other voices on the line. But her mother was well, thank you, a shoe box had arrived by UPS, filled with green paper, and——

"What was that, Mother? I can't hear you!"

"Hello, the house," the deep male voice behind Maeve yelled. She whirled around to find Ash Corbet standing in the doorway, dripping all over her very poor rug. "Shelter before I drown?" he pleaded.

Maeve waved approval, and laughed as he squished down in one of the big armchairs in the van. Water ran out of his shoes; his hair was plastered against his head.

"I said it's more money than I know what to do with," her mother yelled. "What do I do with it?"

"Open a——" Maeve started to say, then stared at Corbet. His head was tilted to one side, paying close attention to what she was saying. Back off, Maeve thought. "Open yourself a bank account," she yelled back to her mother. "And I'll call you again in a few days." Goodnights, words of affection, and she put the instrument down.

"It's cold," she announced, rubbing her hands up and down her forearms. "How can that be, in Florida?"

"Everything is comparative," Corbet said, chuckling. "I don't suppose you could spare me the use of a towel like yours?" Maeve looked down at her towel-wrapped body. She had forgotten how little she was wearing.

"I—yes," she stammered, and scooted down the tiny hall to the bathroom. When she came back she was swathed in a robe that covered her from throat to ankle, with the belt tied securely in a square knot.

He had stripped off his shirt and was standing, waiting for her. There was nothing to be seen that she hadn't seen before down at the beach. He was slender, but well-muscled. A great broth of a boy, her father would have said. His eyes sparkled with humor. A man not un-willing to laugh at himself, Maeve thought. Not a bad thing to have in a male. He took the towel, touching her fingers as he did. She was surprised at the little flicker of electricity that emerged from that touch.

"Bad telephone connection?" he asked as he toweled himself down.

"Terrible," she admitted. "Of course, it was a long-distance call."

"It has nothing to do with long distance," he reported. "It's the cable."

Maeve looked questioningly.

"We only have twelve telephones in the Cove," he explained. "One little cable that goes all the way to Cross City. Get a little moisture in it, and you have all kinds of cross talk. I've seen days when we were all on what seemed to be a party line. But it seldom rains in Florida, of course."

"Of course," she agreed solemnly. "Although I have read newspaper reports on occasion about storms and hurricanes and tornadoes——"

"Only in *Californian* newspapers," he interjected. "So, tell me about your day."

"You wouldn't believe," she said, sighing. "I don't know which are worse—my houses, or the people who live in them."

"You used the wrong words," he chuckled. "Words like 'money.' I hate to admit it, but most of us have been freeloading for some months, you know. I suppose that's all over now?"

"All over," she said glumly. "How else am I going to get the roofs fixed?"

"Why, we all thought that you had more than enough money," he reported. "After all, to buy the whole settlement?"

"It was a bargain," she said. "A real bargain. You'd be surprised how glad that Mr. McCormac was to receive a cash offer. Ever heard of him?"

"Shamus McCormac? Why don't we adjourn to the kitchen and I'll tell you all about it?" The offer was too enticing. Maeve was dying for a decent cup of coffee— meaning one that someone else made for her—and if there was anything about Uncle Shamus to be learned . . . well, why not? And while I'm at it, she told herself as she followed him down the hall, let's find out something more about *this* impossible man at the same time. Beowulf seemed to be reading her mind. He offered a very sharp "woof" and joined the procession.

"No, I only met this McCormac fellow a couple of times," Ash said as he sipped at his coffee. "Once here in the Cove, and the other time over in Gainesville. Small, round, a ruddy complexion, not much hair on the top of his head, and small blue eyes. You know, the kind of eyes that seem to be saying, 'Don't believe anything my mouth tells you. We're not related.' But then, you must have met him?''

"Not really," Maeve told him. "We dealt through a third party."

"Well, he hardly spent twenty minutes at the Cove when he came by, and Rob Stanley is the sort of man who wouldn't tell you the time of day. So why are you interested at this late date?''

And that, Maeve told herself, is something you'll never find out, Mr. Corbet. Time for another approach. "Just curiosity," she murmured. "Just curiosity."

They stared at each other across the table for a moment. Beowulf, restlessly waiting for some tribute from the tabletop, growled. "Pest," Maeve muttered. "Why is it that my dog likes you?"

"If I tell you, you won't like it."

"So, take a chance," she prompted.

"Okay." He leaned back expansively in his chair and one hand scratched at the dog's neck. "Beowulf and I have a couple of things in common."

"Do you really?" A soft murmur of disbelief.

"Really. We're both somewhat mangy creatures, and we both like to be in your vicinity."

"Now wait just a minute," she said angrily. "Don't charge my dog with your own bad habits. Beowulf is a very neat dog—on occasions. And, while I'm at it, Mr. Corbet, why is it that I'm always bumping into you in strange places? Every time I turn around I seem to find you following me. That *is* what you're doing, isn't it? Following me?''

He threw up both hands in surrender, laughing all the while. "Not guilty," he told her, "but it's only because I didn't think of it. I believe I'll take up Mae tracing for a living."

He might not have realized how sensitive she was to those sorts of words, Maeve thought, but then again...

"Why?" she asked.

"Why?" he laughed again. "Don't you ever look in the mirror? You're a lovely lady, especially when you're angry. That little touch of red in your cheeks adds just the right amount of color. Any man in the world with a little red blood left in his veins would want to follow you. Any of them ever catch you?"

"Nobody," she said primly. "And you're not going to break my record."

"Say, that *is* a challenge," he replied as he scraped his chair back and stood up. Beowulf, uneasy at the tension in the air, backed off into a corner.

"It's stopped raining," she told him. "You might as well run for home, Mr. Corbet."

"Stopped raining? You must be from out-of-state," he said, chuckling. "Lady, it's coming down out there in sheets!"

"Use a little imagination. Imagine you've an umbrella."

"Not my line." He was circling the table, and once again she was backing off.

"Then try a little speed," she snapped. "Run between the raindrops—and don't you dare kiss me. There's been enough of that going around lately! It's some damned virus running through this house."

"Ah, but you like it," he murmured.

"Darned if I don't," she said some moments later when the door had slammed behind him. "But I don't intend to make a habit out of it!"

Maeve was up early the next day. There were a couple more companies in New Orleans who wanted her service;

she managed to contact each of them through her computer, furnishing her new address. Each presented her with a problem requiring quick resolution. There were some difficulties. Someone else was sending out computer tones, which were splashing over on to her line. She had to ask twice for repeats.

There was no fancy breakfast waiting; last night she had, for the first time, locked all her doors against intrusion. "But cornflakes aren't bad," she told Beowulf as she tried to feed him some. He complained at length, but did condescend to lick the milk out of the dish. "You could learn to like them." The dog growled. "That's all that's on offer," she told him finally, and started to study her checklist of houses.

Packy had included not only a normal summary of the contents of each house, but a few additional suggestions. The Jefferson house had a strange oversupply of paintings in stock, almost as if they were copyists. The Wilsons, on the other hand, possessed only a ream of paper and a battered old typewriter, which might explain why he was not too well-known in the writing business.

And Ash Corbet seemed to have more computers, and less time to use them, than anyone in the settlement. He also rented the biggest house in the Cove. Curious, Maeve thought. Certainly not for his law business. If there *is* a smuggler at Smugglers Cove, it doesn't necessarily *have* to be Rob Stanley! She toyed with the idea for longer than she wanted to. The sun had come back with the new morning, and just for once Maeve wanted to get out into it all.

Her binoculars were stuffed down behind the second seat in her van. She dug them out. "Bird watching," she told Beowulf. The big dog grumbled and rolled over on his other side. "So stay home and guard the house," she snapped. The animal barely lifted his head as she stomped out of the door, grabbing at her ancient straw hat as she went.

There was a smidgen of truth in what she had said. She was fond of birds. Not knowledgeable, but fond. Besides which, she told her secret self, there's still one house in the Cove I haven't seen: Rob Stanley's. It was situated around the curve, behind Watch Hill, and she had not before found a good excuse to peek and pry. So, covered by her camouflage jumpsuit, walking boots, and straw hat, she went out into the sunshine to attack the back side of the hill, not realizing that there were other sets of binoculars in the settlement, one pair of which were trained on her as she fumbled her way up the hill.

It was a hard climb. Not that Watch Hill was a tremendously high peak; in a land of flat plains and swamps anything over one hundred feet could almost be called a mountain. The problem, rather, was that the east side was a jumble of massive rocks, requiring that her straight path to the top wind back and forth like the marks of a child's shoes in freshly laid cement.

In any event, she was worn to the bone, perspiring like mad, and just a little put out when she threw herself down on a patch of grass just below the top of the hill. "Nice girls don't sweat," she lectured herself. "Nice girls bring a can of water with them when they climb mountains." She looked around. The view was magnificent. The Gulf was quiet, sparkling. Only the gulls were aloft, one group circling the Cove's rubbish dump, the other far out at sea, concentrating on what must be a reef. Bird watching, she teased herself. "Bah! *Stupid* girls end up perched on a rock in the hot sun, with their full canteen of water sitting back down there on the kitchen table! So, who's wiser, me or Beowulf?''

It wasn't the sort of question she wanted to debate. She dropped onto her back, shaded her eyes, and rested. Unfortunately, although her body was prepared to rest, her mind was not. Things were bothering her. Not her Uncle Shamus, nor her partner Packy, nor smuggler-good guy Stanley, but rather the enigma, Ash Corbet. Just suppose he *was* a lawyer? That wasn't exactly a recommendation. The jails were full of crooked lawyers; it was to be supposed that there was an equal number uncaught, running around the countryside. And yet— why all this patented eagerness to kiss me? Or, vice versa, why do I get such a startling reaction when he does? The truth of the matter, Maeve McCormac, is that you *like* to be kissed by him. And where is it written that women only fall in love with the ''good guys''?

The whole argument was too much for her. She rolled over on her stomach, inched her way up to the crest of the hill, and stared down. And immediately crossed the Stanley house off as the place where all those bottles of wine might have ended up, way back in the nineteen-twenties. The house was a modern stone and wood marvel, sprawled across the hillside, with huge glass windows peering out to sea. Cathedral windows, she thought. And a large porch outside, also to seaward. A modern design; surely the house could not be more than twenty years old, and thus out of the running.

The idea bothered her. To be truthful, she *wanted* Stanley to be the bad guy. Why? Because that would mean that Ash Corbet was *not*.

Disgusted with her own torpid reasoning, she pulled the binoculars out of their case and focused them on the birds at sea. It was not a reef, her glasses revealed. The birds in that further flock were hustling free feeds from a fishing boat, anchored about a quarter of a mile off shore. Not a small boat, by any means, but a ninety-footer, designed as a stern trawler. But not towing its nets. It just sat there at anchor, with a couple of its crew members stretched out on the forward deck, enjoying life.

"Damn!" Maeve snorted. Everything she did at the Cove seemed to turn into *another* mystery. Why would a trawler be anchored so near to shore? Waiting? For what? Disgusted, she turned her binoculars on the Stanley house. Brought closer, it appeared even more imposing. More glass than common sense, and topped by what appeared to be a recent addition, a glassed-in watchtower at the very peak of the house.

Her glasses wandered, down to the ground floor, which was itself some fifty feet above the level of the sandy beach. A hundred feet off the beach the Stanley yacht tugged at anchor. A high-powered gleaming boat of some forty feet, it could be classified as a "cigarette boat," a long thin pencil of power, prepared to run at high speed over a great many miles. No wonder Rob wanted a better anchorage. That was one expensive piece of shipping, and anchored on a dangerous lee shore!

So at least that's one puzzle solved, she told herself. Rob Stanley is one of the good guys, right? Her binoculars wandered back to the house. Along the edge of the ground floor was a wooden veranda, open to the skies. There was Rob himself, sitting on the beach lounge, holding a glass in his hand. And next to him, half hidden by a large beach umbrella, was another figure.

Maeve could barely see an arm, covered with bright cloth. His mother, no doubt. There hardly seemed to be anyone else stirring in all the house. Confirmation? Rob and his mother?

"Well, so here's where you're hiding!" Maeve almost jumped off the mountain, so startled was she. Inching up beside her was Ash Corbet.

"Good Lord, what are you doing here?" she sputtered.

"You forgot your canteen," he announced, passing her the battered water container. "It just won't do. You could become dehydrated—or whatever they call it."

"Don't give me that," she muttered. "You damn lawyers know *all* the words. How did you know where I was?"

"I hate to inform on a friend," he said, chuckling. "Have a drink. The water's still cold. I never ever knew a girl who could get angry as quickly as you can. Take a sip."

"Drop dead," she returned bitterly. "I don't take orders." But her throat was parched, and it hardly seemed a wise idea to cut off her nose to—whatever that cliché was. The water gurgled satisfactorily down her throat. "Thank you," she said, not meaning it at all.

"How gracious," he returned. "Your mother's only child?"

"How did you know?"

"Even a mother couldn't put up with two like you." As soon as he made the announcement he rolled away from her, and the palm of her hand smacked a very stubborn rock, rather than his cheek, and brought a pain-tear to her eye.

"Hey, I didn't mean——" He was back at her side again, solicitously, dabbing at her cheek with a massive handkerchief that had appeared like magic. "I didn't mean to insult you," he said, sighing. "I'm not as well trained as you are. My mother would be ashamed of me."

"Oh? You have a mother?"

"Doesn't everyone?"

"I have had a suspicion for some years about some people," she told him grimly. "I'm not crying because of anything you said. I'm crying because I *wanted* very badly to hit you, and I missed, and the rock was hard. Now, could you kindly go away and leave me to my bird watching?"

"So *that's* what you're doing." He moved closer, well within her personal space. She shifted uneasily, but one of his arms came over her and held her in place. "Hush, now," he murmured. "Your birds are a-wing."

"If you think you're Sherlock Holmes," she returned, "forget it. Basil Rathbone will always be my ideal Holmes." There was no answer. She looked up at him. He had seized her binoculars and was studying the house below intently.

"What are you doing?" she gasped.

"Bird watching."

She tried to move, but his powerful arm held her glued to the ground, only able to move her head. She struggled a bit more, and then gave up. "That's not fair. Those are my binoculars."

"And your birds," he murmured, handing her property back to her, and releasing the pressure so she could get her head and arms up. The glasses needed refocusing. She fussed with the knobs until the veranda below sprang into sharp focus.

"It's only Rob and his mother," she told him indignantly.

"Is that a fact?"

"Of course it's a fact," she snapped. "I think you must be involved in a lot of nefarious schemes; you're always thinking the worst of—— Oh, my!"

"See something interesting?"

"I—er—Lord," she muttered, her mind all asunder. Another one of her great solutions had come apart at the seams. Rob Stanley's mother, a rotund figure in black trousers and an aloha shirt, had just turned to say something to her son. She had a large gray mustache and a Vandyke beard!

"Oh, my," Maeve gulped again. The pressure was off her back. She turned around to look. Ash Corbet was up on one knee, focusing a small camera—with the largest lens Maeve had ever seen. His fingers clicked, once, twice.

"Something wrong?" he asked as he lowered the camera and grinned down at her.

"Who——?" she started to say, and then changed to 'What—— ?" And then stopped and took a deep breath. "He said he lived with his mother," she finally stammered. "With his mother! Do you suppose he's one of *those* kinds of——?"

"Not hardly," Corbet reported as he dropped down beside her. "No, he's not one of—'those kinds of men.' It's just that he tends to lie on occasion."

"Then you know something about what's going on around here," she said in a demanding voice.

"As little as possible," Ash told her. "It doesn't pay to know too much. Haven't you found that out, little girl?"

"I—don't believe it. What about Stanley?"

"What about him? Why should I tell you anything about Rob Stanley? He has nothing to do with a computer consultant."

"But—he wants to buy my land. He wants to buy my pier. He wants to——"

"My, he has a lot of wants, hasn't he?" A pause, while he ran his eye over her face. A blush-red face, marked by anxiety. "Maybe I could tell you a little something? Keep away from him. He's a small-time developer who is getting himself into big-time trouble!"

"Your kind of trouble?"

His head snapped around. Those gentle eyes turned hard as flint. She was lying on her back. His arm and part of his weight came over on her, and his face filled her field of vision.

"And just what do you know about my kind of trouble?" A cold question, from cold eyes, which missed not a bit of her attempt to swallow. Suddenly Ash Corbet had become something beyond her comprehension.

"I don't know a thing," she muttered. "Not a thing. I just said that. It just came out. Honestly." She tried to draw away from him, but there was nowhere to go. A huge rock pinned her down on one side, and his weight on the other. He seemed to have become ten feet tall and five hundred pounds of agitated weight. "Nothing," she repeated weakly.

"I'm glad to hear that." For a moment or two he appeared not too glad about anything, but then he smiled and the tension broke. "I need to know something about Mary Kennedy," he said.

"There's nothing to know," she offered tentatively. "Nothing. I told you. I was born in Georgia twenty-six years ago. I went to school. We moved to Apalachicola. My mother lives there. I do computer work. End of report. Now, how about you? How did you ever become a deputy sheriff, for goodness' sakes?"

Out of all that mass of misinformation he seemed to zoom in on the essential point. "Twenty-six? A nice age. I went by that milestone a time or two ago."

He paused, but Maeve was not about to let him get off the subject. There was so much she wanted to know—and had no idea why. "How many times ago?" she insisted.

"Ah. If that's what you want," he said, laughing, "I'm thirty-four years old, unmarried. I was born and brought up in Lafayette County, and earned my law degree at the University of Florida. Oh, and I'm a Baptist by persuasion. Now, what else did you want to know?"

"How did you get to be a deputy sheriff?" she half whispered.

"Influence," he responded promptly. "I'm not a very good lawyer, but my father had a number of friends around these parts. Pure political influence. Anything else?"

"And you think I should believe all that? Who was that man with Rob Stanley?"

"That man? I'm not sure I know. That's why I took his picture. As for the rest, you might as well believe," he said. "Some of it's true."

"Which part?"

"My, you are determined, Mary Kennedy. I'll leave you to find out that for yourself. Now, I know you'd like to sit up here and watch the birds some more, but I've got business to attend to. You'll excuse me?" He slid back down off the crest of the hill and sat up.

"No. I—wait." She backed off and joined him, out of sight of the house—and the sea gulls for that matter. He grinned at her again.

"Which—I mean—is Ash Corbet your real name?"

"Absolutely." Another quick grin and he was up on his feet, brushing dirt off his jeans. "Believe it. Corbet is as much my name as Kennedy is yours." With which he went off down the hill, whistling.

He's a very poor whistler, Maeve told herself. His name is Corbet just as truly as mine is Kennedy. Good Lord, do you suppose he knows something? Almost out of sight now, Ash turned and waved to her. Maeve waved back. Did he know he was leaving a very confused woman behind him, near the top of Watch Hill?

CHAPTER FIVE

CHAMBERS IMPORTING of Gulfport, Mississippi was hardly getting its money's worth. Maeve sorted restlessly through the reams of paper containing the company's faulty computer program. Her usually keen mind was on strike, or something. Or so she told herself as she nibbled her lip and sipped from her coffee mug. It was getting better. The coffee, that was. All it had taken was a little more care and concern, a careful measurement of the freeze-dried coffee into the same sized mug— *et voilà!* Or whatever. And, of course, nobody could spoil toast. Strange how it had taken her all these many years to discover such simple truths.

Her mother had lectured at her, scolded her, teased her—to no avail. But Ash Corbet required only a few minutes of demonstration, and the Gordian knot was cut. Ash Corbet. Miracle man or con artist deluxe? She hardly knew the answer because of all the confusion in her mind. Uncle Shamus? Where in God's world could he be? He had sold off the pier and the land surrounding it, and disappeared. Surely sooner or later he would be back to get rid of the rest of the Cove? Rob Stanley? Why did he want the pier? How was it that his "mother" had turned out to be a man? And Ash Corbet. Why am I so...uncomfortable in his presence? No, that wasn't the word. *Uneasy*—that was more like it. The man's face kept popping up in her memory, wiping out everything more important than he. And not many things ranked in *that* category!

A thoroughly objectionable man, who went around kissing people without their consent! Even that thought gave her a little jab. Does he go around kissing *people*, or just me? I couldn't stand it if I found he's really operating on the wholesaler kissing level. On the other hand... Her mind shied away from the thought to follow, and then came back to gnaw at it. On the other hand, I haven't objected all that much to the kissing, have I? Maeve shook her head in disgust—at herself—and fingered the papers in front of her. She had known an average number of eligible young men in her life, kissed more than a few of them, almost shared the back seat of a parked car once, to her chagrin. But none of them had been so—palatable as Ash. Ashley, she had thought his name to be, only to hear from others that it was Ashton.

Ashton Corbet. Mrs. Ashton Corbet? Her cheeks turned brilliant red at the thought, and she immediately pushed it away, gave herself a strong lecture, and really began to concentrate on the problem before her. As a result, Chambers Importing happily received the solution to its difficulties in jig time, and promised an immediate swelling of her bank account. But that only raised another problem.

When Packy came by for coffee he brought his own bagels for toasting, and she mentioned the problem. "The only *big* banks are in Gainesville," he allowed. "Fifty or sixty miles. If you're talking big money, it's best not to put no strain on a new identity, you know. Go to the biggest place around, act like you was important. You know, accordin' to the Federal Law, them banks have to report to the Feds any movement of money at ten thousand dollars or above. That's to catch up on them money launderers. Tell you what, I'll make up some letterheads under the name of—oh—Kennedy Enterprises Incorporated?"

"Oh, Lord," Maeve sighed. "Couldn't it just be Mary Kennedy?"

The old man chuckled as he bit into his toasted bagel. "You ain't never gonna be able to work a successful con," he said mournfully, as if his best student had just flunked out of class. "You got no idea, have you? Look. Mary Kennedy is a nice name. You got a nice honest face. But banks and businesses, they look at things like Kennedy Enterprises Incorporated and they see guarantees and boards of directors, and things like that, and if it don't open their hearts, it does open their wallets."

"You're saying people are gullible, aren't you?"

"Now there you go. Your first successful lesson," he agreed. "People are gullible. So I print the letterheads, you write to the First Bank and tell them you're coming, and they wheel out the band for you, and that's one more nail to your new self, lady."

"Okay, okay," Maeve said, shaking her head dolefully. The more you struggle toward shore, the deeper the water gets, she told herself. And then another thought came. "Packy, I'm going to have to put you on a salary. What in the world are you living on? Savings?"

"Salary?" he exclaimed. "You mean like holdin' a job? I ain't never held no job. Not in all my years. No regular job, that is. I get along now on Social Security checks," he reported proudly. "Like most of the people in the Cove. So I'll be off and print those letterheads right quick. No ideas about the wine yet, I suppose?"

"Not a glimmer," she returned. "Are you sure the stuff's not dumped in the swamp? It starts only three hundred yards to the back of here."

"Looked there for years," he said gloomily. "Well, I better get packin'. Let me tell you somethin', Mary Kennedy. You ain't made progress on my problem, but you surely lighten up life in these parts."

"Oh, Packy," she sighed, and walked him to the door. At which point she kissed him gently on his lined forehead, and he walked out in something of a daze.

"Hey!" said the man she loved to hate. He was leaning against the side of the house, back to denim shorts and a ragged shirt. "Packy, you old goat, what the devil are you doing? That's *my* girl, and I don't look too happily on other guys kissing *my* girl!!"

"You jus' talking through your ear," the old man chuckled. "Wanna get kissed around here, you got to stand in line." He tipped Ash Corbet a wink and made off down the path.

"Well, I take that mighty poorly, ma'am," the slim dark-haired man complained as he lounged up to the door.

"I don't see why you should," Maeve commented as she made to shut the screen door. His big foot was in the way. She hadn't noticed before how much of him was turned under to make feet. "You don't have any bragging rights on me, Mr. Corbet."

"I aim to do something about that pretty quick," he assured her. "Well, one of these days real soon. There's a country dance at the community center tonight. Want to go dancing with me?"

"Country dancing?"

"Square dancing," he explained. "Form up squares and four hands around, down the line and docie doe?"

"I—I'm afraid you've got the wrong girl," she said. She sounded sorrowful, and truly was. For no good reason that she knew of, she was sure she'd love to go dancing with this annoying damned man. Just to step on his toes, she assured herself. Nothing more.

"So you could learn," he suggested. "All very simple, you know. Come on, Mary Kennedy. I'll pester you all day if you hold out on me. Think how much easier it would be just to say yes."

"That's probably the best reason you've come up with since I moved here." It was impossible to keep a straight face when talking to this impossible man. A giggle escaped her, quickly suppressed.

"I'll take that for a yes." He grinned down at her again, a big broad friendly grin that almost snatched her breath away. In just that one instant Ash Corbet, Ash the Objectionable, had become a *very* interesting man! "Eight o'clock," he said, pulling back his shoe from out of the doorjamb. "And I thank you for not slamming the door on my foot the way you wanted to."

He ambled off, like some big country boy following the cows. His hands were in his pockets, and his whistling hadn't improved an iota, but *something* had changed, she told herself.

Maeve came out on the back porch and shaded her eyes with one hand, the better to watch him walk away down the path, around the corner of the Hiller house, and thus out of sight. Am I so easy to read? she asked herself. How could he know that I would have slammed the door on him? She gave herself a mental shake. Life is too complex, too dangerous, to allow perfect strangers to read my mind! And then, as an afterthought, well, he's not all *that* perfect.

Maeve was still talking to herself as she dressed, shortly before eight that night. She definitely had *no* intention of going to a dance with that man; she was only dressing nicely so that she could decline his invitation at the door. There might be others watching, and Maeve McCormac felt the need to impress the citizens. So the wide-swirling red peasant skirt, the white dirndl blouse, low and square-cut to show the upper swell of her not inconsiderable breasts, and a yellow ribbon to tie in her auburn curls. And, just in case something else should come up, a sensible pair of flat dancing shoes and a Paisley shawl.

"Magnifique!" he exclaimed as she came to the door. She blushed prettily. "And all ready to go. I like that. Most women believe it's protocol to make a man wait. But not you."

"No——" she started to say, and then swallowed the rest of the words. He seemed so happy to see her on time that she could hardly tell him she was early in order to say she wasn't coming at *all*! That would be the height of unseemliness. And so she said nothing more to him, but did threaten Beowulf with mayhem if he failed to guard the house while she was away. Her dog recognized that he was being verbally abused because she didn't dare to take it out on Ash Corbet, and tactfully ignored the whole affair.

There was a quarter moon edging the darkness, and a cool breeze coming in off the Gulf. She stumbled as she stepped down off the porch; his big hand steadied her, so it seemed acceptable that they walk over to the hall hand in hand.

Maeve could hear the music a block away. Two or three fiddles, a guitar, a set of drums, all in the foot-tapping rhythm of country music. Ash towed her up the steps of the community building, and through the wide-open double doors. "Air-conditioning," Carrie Wilson told them as she greeted them at the door. "Good to see you, Mary." The presence of the motherly figure relieved some of Maeve's tensions. Made the evening seem almost real.

"And you," Maeve yelled over the noise from within. "All the children bedded down for the night?"

"Not hardly. I hired a sitter. Along about ten o'clock I'll send their father home to put them away. See, men are good for some things. But you be careful, Mary. This Ash Corbet is a noted rake." She obviously didn't mean it, for she took Ash's arm and hugged him genially, just as the music pounded to a stop. "There, now. I've got to find my husband. He's always chasing the girls!" She waved her hand in the direction of a tall bald man of uncertain age, who was surrounded by four white-haired women.

"Don't look as if he's pining away for you," Ash commented. Carrie Wilson made a face at him, and went laughing across the floor. "And now we'll dance," Ash announced.

"But—I told you, I don't know square dancing," Maeve protested.

"So we'll fake it," he told her as he folded her up into a little package in his arms. The band struck up a waltz. Waltzing she knew. As did he.

They joined the throng circling the room, a perfect match for each other in step and wit and desire. Flaming desire, Maeve told herself as she buried her face in the folds of his linen shirt. Lord, what am I doing? Wasn't the kissing enough?

Apparently it wasn't. Not for him nor for her. He pulled her across the inches that separated them, and treasured her against his full length. One misstep by either of them would have sent them skidding to the floor.

"We make a fine match," he said as they completed their first swing around the small hall. And Maeve could not deny it. Her feet performed, while her mind rose high above the throng in exultation. Just for those lovely moments, thief or lawyer or no-good, she loved him. A shiver ran up and down her spine. She put the fear firmly behind her, rested in his arms, and let the dream continue.

The music stopped before they did. There was a giggle or two from the crowd watching as the pair of them, the only couple left on the floor, circled to their own beat. She murmured an objection when he slowed them to a stop, and then blushed as she realized the music had all been in her heart. A round of applause greeted them. He laughed, she blushed, and they both fled to the shelter of the refreshment table.

The interval was filled with entertainment. Clowns, a stand-up comic, and then, to Maeve's amazement, Ash Corbet and a magic act that filled the hall with laughter. Sleight of hand was his speciality, a clumsy sort of misdirection that seemed to be so easily spotted, but actually so skillfully done that the audience was wrong every time. It bothered Maeve for a moment; not that everyone was laughing at him, but rather how she had missed that smoothness of hand and mind before. Seen it, but not recognized it for what it was. So, Ash Corbet is *not* the ignorant country boy, she told herself, and firmly marked it down in her memory!

There was another waltz one hour later, and in the meantime Maeve received lessons and coaching from half a dozen men, all eager to partner her in the forming squares. But when the waltz sounded, and Ash Corbet appeared, Maeve was panting for breath.

"Hot in here," he said, chuckling, as he gathered her up in his arms.

"What happened to——?"

"Those other guys? They decided they needed a rest. Or their wives needed them. Or one I had to threaten with a broken nose."

"You didn't!"

They were standing there, almost glued together. The other couples were already swirling around; Maeve and Ash were just standing in one place, swaying to the music, arms around each other. "You have no idea to what lengths I'll go," he said solemnly—and swept her out into the circling throng again.

It was a repetition of her first experience. A moment of heady delight, warning fire signals running up her back, lovely dreams. Mrs. Ashton Corbet. Fleeting moments of grace and joy, not a word spoken between them. But this time, when the music stopped, so did he, with an apologetic smile. And no sooner did he release her than Rob Stanley was in front of her, offering.

"I'm really out of breath," she stammered. "I——"

"Well then, let's go out on the porch and cool off," he suggested. He tucked her hand under his arm, and she went along reluctantly, looking over her shoulder, unable to find where Ash had vanished to.

The porch was bigger than she had expected, extending all the way around the building; and more popular than she had thought. It took more than a moment or two to find a clear space in one far corner. Rob Stanley was an enthusiastic place hunter. By the time he'd ploughed to a stop, Maeve was even more short of breath. But there was a wooden bench in the corner, and she sank onto that and inhaled deeply.

"You really *were* tired," the big man commented as he sat down beside her. Maeve offered him a smile, and looked around her. They were on the side of the building facing the water. The Gulf winds were light, and the moon created a path across the rippling water, one so well-marked that Maeve half dreamed she could walk it. But when she mentioned that to Stanley he was unable to grasp her meaning, and she changed the subject.

"Do you come to all these dances?" she asked.

"No. Not really. I'm not really part of the Cove culture," he said. She could hear the disdain in his voice. I'm not one of these scruffy artists, it said.

"Yes, of course, I realize that." Maeve did her best to sound sincere. It was a hard effort, and poorly done, but Stanley did not notice.

"Scruffy bunch of people," he continued. "Makes you wonder why they all ended up at the Cove."

Maeve, who was willing now to defend her settlement, frowned at him. "I suppose they are looking for peace and quiet. Artists, in whatever field, need that sort of thing. Add on to it the beach and the sunshine, and I suppose it's just what's needed."

"Soft heart, Mary," he commented. "Soft heart. They'll do you out of your eyeteeth, you know. You'd be better off selling the whole place."

"And who do you think might make me an offer?" she asked. I'm behaving like a lawyer, she told herself. Rule number one: never ask a question if you don't know the answer beforehand.

"Why, to tell the truth," Rob said unctuously, "I'm a member of a little syndicate that might be glad to take it off your hands." The air hung heavy with the unsaid question mark. And evict everybody, she told herself.

Throw them all out, bag and baggage, and tear down the whole place!

"I don't think I'm ready to make such a commitment. I'd have to think it all over. How are you coming along about the pier?"

"Had my crew start shoring it up this afternoon," he returned. If he was disappointed, he was not about to show it. The sign of a good salesman, Maeve told herself. Don't overcrowd the customer. "And we'll start on the wall tomorrow."

"There surely isn't any reason to hurry on the wall? Won't it take months to reverse the tidal action and deepen the channel?"

"Months and months," he agreed jovially. "But you have to start somewhere. You'll see. It will make a nice place for my boat, and do a little something for your community."

I'm sure it will, Maeve thought. A *very little* something. But he's willing to spend a great deal of money just for a place to tie up his yacht. Who knows? Boat owners are strange people. You have to be a *rich* nut to support the purchase of a boat like his. And that makes him—a sharp developer? Except for——

"How's your mother?" she asked pointedly. He might have been surprised by the question, but he failed to show it.

"Much better," he responded. "She left today. To go to see my brother, as I mentioned to you before." And that, Maeve thought, confirms his status. If there's a smuggler somewhere, this one isn't he. On the other hand, he's the only remote connection I have with Shamus McCormac, wherever he may be.

Behind her, inside the hall, the band struck up again with another waltz. Maeve took a quick look at her wristwatch. Eleven-thirty, so soon? The night had fled. She had written her letter to the bank and deposited it in the sub-post office at the general store. She had dropped Rob Stanley out of the mystery equation, and that left her only Shamus's thievery, Packy's wine, and Corbet's enigma. She turned to Rob, who seemed to be watching her like a hawk.

"So this is where you've gotten to." Ash Corbet stood in front of her, bending slightly, extending both hands in her direction. "You promised me this dance."

"The lady and I are talking," Stanley grumbled as he stood up. Maeve compared them as they stood confronting each other. Stanley was bigger, beefier, like a broadsword ready for combat. Ash was lean, almost as tall, like a rapier, poised and ready. She remembered those moments in his arms, and the music swayed her judgment.

"Yes, I did," she murmured, and accepted the hands. Corbet tugged her to her feet and started to tow her away. "I enjoyed the talk," she called back over her shoulder. "Don't forget the contract for the lease of the pier."

"I won't," Stanley said, but by that time she was at the corner, and moments later in Ash Corbet's arms, and the fantasy played again as music and man swept her mind away together. At midnight the band featured a roll on the drums and the clash of cymbals, and peppered the night air with, "Good night, ladies."

Ash walked her home, not hand in hand this time, but rather arm in arm. The moonlight, flickering behind scurrying clouds, painted a dreamy silver mosaic over the dull grey of the settlement, and when he kissed her—wasn't that supposed to be the price for an evening of dancing?—he flavored the night and sent her to bed with her mind whirling.

* * *

The night of the dance, and all its attendant meanings, kept bursting intermittently into Maeve's mind for the next few days. But the rain that came early that next morning, sweeping into her living room through an open window, left a more prosaic problem. Something smelled.

"I hate to tell you this," Ash Corbet said as he set aside his breakfast plate at her kitchen table.

"Well, don't, then," Maeve muttered. "I've enough bad news on my plate to last for weeks. Why is it that you seem to be living here? Every morning when I get up, here you are."

"It's called courting," he said, and grinned at her.

"In the earliest morning, for goodness' sakes?"

She sounded exasperated, but wasn't. It had become a pleasure to share breakfasts with the man. And today *she* had cooked it all, and he hadn't once choked on anything! He not only was a good teacher, but a good conversationalist. He could talk about anything in the world at the drop of a hat. Anything except Ash Corbet, that was. And although he was a little behind in computer programming techniques he *did* display considerable knowledge about what computers were all about. For the rest, "I'm a painter," he kept insisting when she nagged at him. "A true artist. Surely you don't expect to hear anything more than that?"

Maeve put both elbows on the table and glared at him. "What's this I hear about painting by numbers?" she enquired.

"A dirty lie," he said. "Tell me who said that and I'll paint his eyes out. Who?"

"I have my sources," she giggled. "More than one. And, by the way, how did that fellow make out up at

Cross City? The one you were defending for wife beating?''

He might not have been an artist, but he certainly was an actor. He shook his head sadly. "Poor man. I'm sure you and the rest of womankind will be happy. I lost the case hands down, and the judge—the female judge, mind you—sent him away for twelve months."

"He deserved it," she crowed.

"For beating his wife! Twelve months for beating his wife? She probably deserved a beating anyway!"

"No," she chuckled. "For hiring such a lousy lawyer!"

"Well, a lot *you* know," he offered morosely. "That's the trouble with the law business. Everyone expects you to win!"

"So, tell me," she teased, "how many cases have you won this last year?"

"Unfair," he returned, finishing off his coffee. "It's been a bad year."

"None, huh?"

"I hate women who keep score," he returned, his nose elevated in a holier-than-thou attitude. "Just for that, I'll tell you what's wrong in this house whether you like it or not!"

"Typical male attitude," she giggled "Go ahead. Make my day."

"It's your rug in the living room," he pontificated. "I'll bet it's been there since the house was built. It got wet in the rain, and that's what you smell."

"I find that hard to believe," she said. "Fifty years or more?"

"The one in *my* house was identical to that thing you have on your floor," he told her, "and when I hired a fellow to take it up it reduced the air pollution inside immensely.''

"You *hired* someone to take up a rug?''

"Surely did. We painters have delicate constitutions.'' She looked him over carefully. If there was any part of his constitution that appeared delicate, Maeve McCormac wasn't able to locate it.

"Then I guess I'll have to do the same,'' she sighed. "But I have a problem about money.''

"Not having any?''

"Oh, I've got some money, but I've got to get over to Gainesville and open a bank account. I think I need to buy a small used car, too. I can't just pull the van away and drive it over there. I thought I might find some little vehicle that I could tow behind the van when I leave.''

"You couldn't move the van without knocking the house down,'' he said solemnly. "Well, how about if I solve both your problems? I'll help you pull up the rug— for a price. And then tomorrow I have to drive over to Gainesville myself, and I could easily accommodate you. Bargain?''

That uneasy feeling crept over her again. "Don't weave too many people into your new identity,'' Packy kept saying. "Crowds are okay; don't let individuals get too close.'' And beyond that, she told herself, too much of Ash Corbet and I could—fall in love? Remember the night of the dance? But we're only talking about pulling up a rug, and a sixty-mile drive, for goodness' sakes. Don't make a major romance out of things like that!

"Yes,'' she answered eagerly. "It's a bargain. The rug is——''

"I know,'' he said. "Just follow my nose?''

"I hope you can work as well as you talk," she challenged him, and led the way into the living room. Beowulf, who knew what the word *work* meant, and didn't care for it in the least, brushed his way through the outward-swinging screen door and played least in sight.

For an hour they struggled. The carpet, whatever its age, had been fitted wall to wall and tacked down on its outer edges. By dint of much scraping, a couple of wounded fingers, and more muscle than common sense, the pair of them managed to loosen the entire structure, only to find it falling to pieces in their hands as they tried to roll it up. In the end Ash picked up handfuls, and carried it out on to the back porch, where Maeve, holding her nose against the odour, stuffed the remnants into plastic bags for the inevitable trip to the town rubbish dump.

Ash went back into the living room with a pair of side-cutting pliers from Maeve's toolbox, and wrestled with the remaining tacks. When she came in to watch he looked up from his hands-and-knees position and grumbled, "It would have been a heck of a lot easier if we'd had a hammer."

"You broke the hammer," she insisted. "With all your wise-guy remarks, you insulted my hammer, and it lost its head, if you'll remember."

"Lord, a punster," he groaned. "I could have fallen in love with a nice girl; instead I get a punster!"

"I *am* a nice girl," she insisted. "And it's not my fault that you—— What did you say?"

But Ash the Ancient knew that he had misspoken, and refused to repeat himself. Instead he flicked a finger at the two middle floorboards under the window. "You've got two nails there," he reported, "that are sticking out far enough to do some damage. You'd better get another hammer and beat them down.''

"Yeah, sure," she told him. The work had been hard, and she was exhausted, sweaty, and just a little peeved. She had forgotten something in the contract negotiations prior to the carpet stripping. "You didn't tell me what it would cost me to have your help in this great enterprise."

He climbed back to his feet and stretched, flexing his very considerable muscles. "Why, so I didn't," he said innocuously, and began to stalk her.

"Hey—just a darned minute," she mumbled, but by that time he had caught up to her, his lips were on hers, her mind went astray, and Beowulf, out on the back steps, howled his complaint.

But Maeve McCormac, who had been very easy to catch indeed, made no complaints at all until long after Ash had turned her loose, promised to be back in the morning for the trip to Gainesville, and had gone whistling down the path. At which time she said to herself and her dog, "He didn't *have* to leave that soon. It's still early in the day!"

And she didn't realize until almost two hours later, as she dreamily worked at cleaning up her kitchen, that he had taken *her* coffee mug with him. It *had* to be hers, and she just couldn't understand. She always added milk in *her* coffee, and the mug left behind contained coffee as black as the Ace of Spades.

In any event, she pottered around for the rest of the day, getting papers and clothing ready for her trip, and went to bed after a cold shower, and dreamed some— delightful—dreams.

CHAPTER SIX

"DIFFERENT car," Maeve announced as she climbed in beside Ash Corbet early the next morning. "Last time you had a Chrysler. Now all of a sudden it's a Ford. You must be made of money."

"Not really," he reported. "I know a used-car dealer. He loans me cars from time to time. I do a little law business for him. Sort of, you wash my back——"

"I know," she interrupted. "There's something collegiate about that. Lawyers and used-car dealers. Birds of a feather?"

"A man has to make a living," he said, sighing. "It's been a bad day so far, Mary, and here you are doing your best to believe the worst about me. Would you rather not go to Gainesville?"

"After all I've gone through?" She shrugged herself down in the seat, smoothing her navy blue skirt around her. Today it was Mary Kennedy Incorporated. Hence the skirt, a matching blazer, a white blouse with lace up the middle, shoes with two-inch heels, and a tan briefcase. Her auburn curls had been brushed to a fare-thee-well, but would resume their usual shape soon enough. "No. I'm sorry, Ash. I apologize and I do want to go today."

"That's better," he acknowledged as he shifted the car into gear. "And your—dog?" She could see his lips form the word "mutt" before he changed his mind. She giggled.

"Beowulf doesn't mind traveling in the van," she told him, "but in smaller vehicles he'd rather stay at home. Besides, I have things to be guarded these days. That's what he's doing. He and Packy."

"Packy too? Becoming fond of the old coot, are you? He makes a good match for the dog, I must say."

Maeve made no answer. She was totally absorbed watching his strong brown hands caress the steering wheel as he guided the car out on to the road. All the skill and magic of the world resided in those hands. The thought sent a little electrical charge up her spine. She was unable to break out of this mesmerizing scene.

"Maeve?" She almost jumped as he prompted her.

"I—what did you say?"

"I merely asked what sort of valuables you have in your house now. As the law in these parts, I ought to know."

"Oh, that. Nothing for the ordinary person to steal," she responded. "But they are valuable to specialists. I have the computer programs for almost a dozen companies in my little lockbox. A normal thief couldn't make beans of them, but a computer thief could. So Beowulf's on guard."

"And Packy."

"Well, yes, but I have a lot more confidence in my dog than my partner."

"Partner?"

She hadn't meant that word to slip out. Which proves again what a lousy conspirator you are, she lectured herself. "It sounds better than employee," she lied. "He's so old, and—well... Look, there are fish jumping out there!"

"Turtles, more than likely," he said, taking a quick squint off into the swamp. "Some nice eating turtles come out of the Suwannee. There are fish too, of course, but not this far out in the backwater. The river suffers from some industrial pollution.''

He seemed to have nothing else to say. Maybe he's one of those drivers who don't wish to be distracted, she thought, and glued her lips together. He's not going to catch me not playing by the rules. Even if I don't know just which rules we have! He cleared his throat as they passed over the main channel of the river near Fanning Springs, but changed his mind about saying anything. He treated the speed limits a little disdainfully when they turned onto highway twenty-four, but what male driver doesn't? she asked herself glumly. And suddenly it was ten o'clock, and they rolled into the county seat of Alachua County, once a trading post known as Hog Town, now a bustling city of almost ninety thousand.

''There's my alma mater,'' he said, waving his hand at the buildings of the University of Florida.

''I'm impressed,'' she offered tentatively. And then he did a wondrous thing. He found a parking space downtown.

''The bank's over there across the street,'' he told her as he checked his wristwatch. ''I'll be up in this building we've parked in front of. How much time will you need?''

''Not much,'' she told him. ''I have to open an account. Half an hour, maybe?''

''Why not?'' he said, chuckling. ''Banks don't make trouble about putting money *in*, it's only when you're trying to take it out that it hurts. I only have a minute or two of business. Suppose I meet you in the bank, say, in fifteen minutes?''

''I'd appreciate that.'' Maeve had traveled many a mile, seen many a strange city, but just at the moment she was suffering from nervous apprehension. She had a feeling, and no sensible woman neglected feelings and intuitions. It would be nice to have this very large man backing her up, just in case. He must have felt the ambience. One of his hands patted hers gently.

"It's only a bank," he offered. "They can't eat you."

"A lot you know," she sighed, and climbed out of the car. He remained behind the wheel, watching her as she navigated the pedestrian crossing. She could feel the weight of his eyes on her back all the way across.

"Yes, our Mr. Frescon will help you," the receptionist told her, and pointed the way to the far corner of the big lobby, where "our Mr. Frescon" turned out to be a shrivelled little fellow, no more than five feet high nor younger than sixty. Mr. Frescon loved forms. He pulled them out from a variety of hiding places and smiled at each and every one of them as if they were his children. "Now then, Mrs.——?"

"Miss," she said very firmly. The Mr. Frescons of this world required firmness. His face fell. "Miss Mary Kennedy, president of Mary Kennedy Enterprises Incorporated. I had my financial officer write to you last week. We want to establish a small checking account to begin with." Mr. Frescon regained his smile and reached for a different form. "Perhaps something on the order of fifty thousand dollars," Maeve added. Said so casually that hardly anyone in the bank could realize it was every penny she had. Mr. Frescon cleared his throat, blinked twice, and put half the forms away. He did everything studiously. Each form was rearranged, put in the proper order, and returned to his desk file with care. Maeve cleared her own throat; there was a lot of that going on these days, and she didn't care for the way things were slowing down.

"You have some identification?" he asked.

"Yes, indeed." She laid one of her business cards squarely in front of him, and then began piling hundred-dollar bills on top of it, in a neat studiously constructed file.

When she went by number fifty the little man wiped the perspiration from his brow and stuttered, "W—well, perhaps there's no need for further identification."

"How nice," Maeve said gently. She upturned her briefcase and let the rest of the cash scatter across his desk, and then added at the top of the pile the last two checks which had come in the mail only yesterday. Then, as Frescon began to wrestle with his forms and his conscience, Maeve sat back in her chair and idly scanned the desks around her.

There was no doubt that her little display had attracted some attention. Two desks away, the clerk *behind* the desk was giving her the eye, while the customer in *front* of the desk had also turned to look more closely; a rotund little man, with a fringe of hair around his bald pate, and the look of an Irish pixie on his full red face. Maeve tasted the description and ran it through her mind one more time. A rotund little man with—— "My God!" she muttered.

"I'll be with you in just a moment, miss." Mr. Frescon had come up out of his paperwork at her comment.

"It's nothing," she assured him, flustered by her own outburst. "Nothing at all. Take all the time you need." Frescon smiled and dived back into his work. The little man at the other desk had turned back to his own work, his face wreathed in smiles. A real con man, Maeve told herself. And at just that moment a big hand fell on her shoulder. She squeaked in alarm and came up fighting, only to find those deep dark eyes and that wide mouth grinning at her.

"I told you I'd join you here," Ash told her. "What's the matter now?"

Maeve dropped back into her chair, aware that she was making an almighty fool of herself. "And that's all that's required," Mr. Frescon was saying. "The money is in a joint investment-checking account, paying——" he stopped to consult a note board near his desk "—paying eight percent interest, compounded monthly. And this is your checkbook. And we'll send the monthly statements to—er—Smugglers Cove?"

The name attracted the attention of the little man at the adjacent desk. He pulled a pair of glasses out of his waistcoat pocket, polished them gently, put them on, and turned his entire attention to Maeve. But he's never seen me before, Maeve told herself frantically. At least I hope he hasn't. Ash followed the direction of her gaze, sized up the little man, then leaned over Frescon's desk.

"That man at the next desk," he asked softly. "Reminds me of someone. Would you happen to know his name?"

Frescon acted as if he had been invited into a gossip conspiracy. "That's one of our newer customers," he half whispered. "Deals with large cash sums all the time. The executor of some estate. Goes by the name of McCormac. Mr. Shamus McCormac."

"Oh, God," Maeve moaned. "Get me out of here, quick. I think I'm going to be sick!" One swipe of Ash Corbet's big hand cleaned up all the papers on the desk and stuffed them into her briefcase. Then his other hand was at her elbow, helping her up.

"Thank you, Miss Kennedy," Frescon blurted out. Maeve muttered something indistinguishable, and found herself being rushed out of the door into the warm fresh air.

"Now, what's up?" Corbet demanded as he led her across the street and injected her into the car. "You're not sick worth a nickel, Mary. Was it that man? That little round fellow? He took an interest in you, believe me. When that clerk of yours blurted out your name the little fellow wrote it down in his notebook. Come on, girl, the guy can't hurt you!"

Maeve had slid across the seat hard up against him. His arm went around her shoulders to comfort her. She leaned forward just far enough to watch the entrance to the bank. "A lot you know," she muttered. "He's already killed me once!"

"One of us," the big man beside her said solemnly, "has been out in the sun too long." After five minutes Shamus McCormac had just come out of the bank and was looking up and down the street. For me, Maeve told herself, and ducked into the protection of Ash's chest. "He's already killed you once?"

"I'm sorry I said that," Maeve responded. "I was excited. I meant—he's already *tried* to kill me once. He's a terrible, terrible man. If I had a gun I'd shoot him right where he stands!" And I mean it too, she told herself excitedly, except I don't know how to shoot a gun, and I don't have one in my purse, and——

"Hey, now," Ash comforted. "You're talking to the law, you know. You want me to—wait here a minute."

"You're not going to arrest him?" A pleading tone. Suddenly it was very important that Ash Corbet not put himself in any danger. He could hear the message behind the words, and his eyes lit up.

"Who, me?" He opened his car door and swung a foot out on the street. "Not only am I the world's worst lawyer, but I'm also a certified coward. Wait here."

Maeve had no difficulty at all in waiting. She ducked her head down onto the seat, completely out of sight, and spent a fruitful ten minutes recalling all the prayers she had learned as a child at her mother's knee. Which meant, of course, that she didn't see Shamus McCormac turn and walk down the street toward a waiting car, nor did she see Ash Corbet beckon a man who had been leaning indolently against the corner of the building, and whisper some sharp commands in the waiting man's ear.

"You can come up for air now," Ash told her as he came back into the car. "The bad man's gone. Tried to kill you, did he? Hard to believe."

Maeve gathered herself up in one piece and sat up as far away from him as she could. "You needn't laugh at me," she remonstrated. "Just because he's not husky and all that doesn't mean he can't be a bad man!"

"No, of course it doesn't," Ash said.

"So why are you laughing, *Mr.* Corbet?"

"Me? Laughing? Perish the thought. I wasn't laughing. I wasn't even *thinking* of laughing. Shamus McCormac, hey? He certainly must deal in a lot of money, that one."

Yeah, Maeve almost said, *my* money!

"You said something?"

"No," she denied. "I—about that car? You were going to take me to that used-car dealer, you know?"

The dealer was friendly indeed. Exceedingly friendly. He seemed to move around Ash Corbet as if he were walking on eggshells. He produced a fine-looking little convertible—and, when Ash frowned at him, admitted that its engine wasn't really all that good. And so down his line, with honesty rampant on a field of blue, until Maeve began to wonder again just what sort of business Corbet was *really* in. "He acts as if you were the local Mafia capo," she hissed at her tall escort when the dealer rushed off to find a better selection.

He looked down at her and grinned. "Do you say so, Mae? Sweet lovable me? I wouldn't hurt a fly."

"No," she spat again, "but how about used-car salesmen?"

"Ah. That's a whole new ball game," he said, chuckling. "But you've got to have more faith and trust in me, ma'am. After all, you're my girl."

"I am not!" Anger boiled, her eyes watered, and she jerked her hand out from under his arm. She managed to get one step away when he caught her and swung her around facing him.

"Now look here," he said gently. "You *are* my girl. When are you going to get that through your head? From now on, every night before you go to bed I want you to say ten times, 'I am Ash's girl.'"

"I would never consider doing such a thing," she snapped. And then, as he tugged her gently closer and leaned down: "No, don't you dare! Not in front of all these people!" That last sentence was more of a wail than a statement, because he wasn't concerned at all about the little group that gathered around and watched and commented on his kissing technique. Which, Maeve admitted later when she had her breath back, was getting better and better.

So much better that, as she drove her new Sprite back towards the Cove, following behind his Ford, she tried the litany out a time or two, just to see how it sounded.

"I am *Ash's* girl. I *am* Ash's girl!" It wasn't true; not in the least true, but it had a delightful ring to it. When she drove up alongside her van she was sorry the trip was over. Her mind was full of plans to make a duet out of the lovely little phrase.

Beowulf was acting strangely. As she stepped out of her little car she could hear him baying. A mournful wail— more of a howl than a bark. Maeve rushed around the house to the back door and tracked him down. The huge old animal was sitting in the corner of the living room, at the window, mourning for all he was worth. The dog could not be backed off a single inch. His huge bottom and tail were hard up against the wall in each direction. Packy was nowhere in sight.

"What is it, love?" Maeve hurried across the room, knelt, and threw her arms around her favorite dog. Beowulf spared her a glance, ran his harsh tongue across her tender nose, and resumed his concert. "What *is* it, love?" didn't seem to work. It was followed by a series of commands, ending eventually with, "Shut up, mutt! You're driving me out of my mind!"

That kind of conversation the dog understood all too well. He came to instant quiet, and followed her meekly out into the kitchen when she commanded. He was so good, in fact, that Maeve was struck with a terrible guilt complex, and fed the dog the steak she had intended for her *own* supper.

And throughout the evening, from time to time, Beowulf would stop whatever he was doing, run into the living room, and whimper until commanded otherwise. At about nine o'clock, under bright moonlight, Maeve decided that the dog was suffering from a lack of exercise, so she whistled him up, picked up his lead, and led him out onto the beach sand. The lead was not for wearing; with her size and weight she could hardly manage if the dog didn't care to obey. Rather, the lead was a reminder of those times when Beowulf was barely a pup, weighing perhaps fifty pounds, and *could* be intimidated!

The entire community was asleep. The only light sparkled from Ash Corbet's house, but Maeve hadn't the nerve to barge into his domestic bliss. Better to let the day end on the romantic note of their trip back to the Cove. So her dog ran, or rather ambled, and Maeve followed along until they came to *her* pier and *her* sea wall.

Rob Stanley had been busier than a hive of bees! New timber gleamed here and there on the long wooden dock, where rotten planks had already been displaced. It almost seemed safe enough to walk on. So they did. A firm rail blocked the seaward end. And squarely in the middle of the fence was a steel pole some six feet high, with a curiously hooded construction on its top. In fact, Maeve had to lean over the rail and look backwards to discover that it was an unlit green warning light, masked so that it could be seen only from the sea, and battery powered since there was no electricity in the Cove.

"Mary? Mary Kennedy?"

Beowulf managed to growl, hardly enough to be called aggressive. A woman stood at the landward end of the pier, waving an arm vigorously. Carrie Wilson, her tall figure clad in trousers and blouse, with a cardigan slung over her shoulders.

"Over here!" Maeve called, unable to repress a grin. Over the course of several days she had met Carrie often, usually at the counters of the general store, and had struck up a friendship with the older woman.

"I thought it was you, Mary. Well, to be honest, I knew it was you because of your dog! What are you doing out here at this time of night?"

"Just looking at the improvements," Maeve returned. "My dog is uneasy for some reason so I thought I'd take him for a run, and look what I've found." She gestured around her at all the work in progress. "And now what are *you* doing out at this hour—without the children?"

"You are looking at the Liberated Woman," Carrie said, giggling. "My husband finished the book and mailed it off this morning. He's earned a vacation, so I waved him off to Disney World at noontime, with all the children. They'll be gone a week."

"*He* gets a vacation by taking *all* the children to——? Wow, what brass you have, Carrie Wilson!"

"Serves him right. You mustn't pamper men, Mary. Why are you fixing up the pier?"

"Me? I'm not. I leased it to Rob Stanley. He wants a place to moor that fancy yacht of his. The water's too shallow over in front of his house. Or so I'm told. How about walking up to the house for a short coffee and a long conversation? I seem to be living entirely in a man's world. I could use some female talk."

"I'll go for that," Carrie agreed. "You have no idea how sick I am of saying 'Eat your spinach' at the dinner table."

"I ought to take notes," Maeve commented. "Some day I might just up and get married."

"Ah?" There was a world of question in the one word. Maeve heard it all and laughed.

"No, I don't have a likely prospect," she added quickly. The two of them walked up the slight incline of sand, chattering inconsequentials; such as the merits, if any, of the few eligible bachelors in the Cove, and the price of clothes for the new season, and cough remedies for babies. All of which had become startlingly interesting to Maeve, although she had never given them a thought before. Carrie, who knew a thing or two herself, was grinning broadly as they came up to the back door and the light fell on Maeve's intense face.

No sooner were they inside the back door than Beowulf made a dash for the living room, and began to howl again. "Listen to that fool dog," Maeve sighed as she followed on, and dragged the protesting animal back out into the kitchen. "I don't know what's going on in his little mind! Sit, Beowulf!"

The dog grumbled and sat, shifting his weight back and forth as if he were balanced on the point of a pin. "It isn't the full moon," Carrie interjected, "so maybe it's love?"

"I doubt that," Maeve returned as she filled the kettle and put it to boil. "We had him—er—altered some years ago. Decaffeinated all right?"

"Let me tell you about..." Carrie began, and all the local gossip came pouring out into Maeve's ears. I didn't know anything like all this was going on, Maeve told herself. I need to pay less attention to computers and more to the world around me!

"And so what do you think?" Carrie had stopped babbling and was looking over at her expectantly.

"Think?" Maeve blushed and fumbled for some answer. "Think about what?"

"Why, about Ash Corbet, of course. Isn't he a doll?"

"Carrie! You forget you're a married woman!"

"With all those kids, I should forget? Listen, sure I'm married, but I'm not dead. I can window-shop with the best of them! He's a very fine young man. More your age, of course, than mine. Do I sound as if I regret that? I don't. My man is the finest in the world, bald head and all, but if I had met Ash twenty-five years ago——"

"He would be eight years old and you'd be yelling 'Eat your spinach' at him," Maeve returned, giggling.

"Spoilsport!" Carrie retorted. "What's the *matter* with that dog?"

Maeve had been using one precautionary hand on Beowulf's collar, but now the dog was squirming and whining, struggling to be free.

"Listen," Carrie said. "I don't know what you do in your house, but there's somebody singing around here. At my best guess, it's a man."

"You're out of your ever-loving mind," Maeve told her. "I—good Lord, there *is* ..." Her hand slipped on Beowulf's collar, and the dog bounded away, back into the living room again.

"I don't like this," Carrie said. "I'm going to get Ash Corbet." She pushed her chair back and started for the door.

"Not him," Maeve pleaded. "I—why don't we just...? I've got my flashlight, and there are two of us, and Beowulf is here. We can handle *anything*."

"I don't know about that. But it's your house. If you're willing, go ahead."

Beowulf was baying again, singing his heart out. Flashlight in hand, Maeve led the procession slowly into the living room. There was nothing too unusual to be seen. Nothing, except a tiny sliver of light peeping out from between the dog's legs. And a ragged man's voice, singing an obscene sea shanty from some distant place.

"Maybe we should have got Ash," Maeve muttered, her hand shaking so much that the light could not be focused on one place.

"Maybe you should have," the man behind them said. Carrie shrieked. Maeve's flashlight clattered to the floor. A much larger beam of light came from the lantern in Ash Corbet's hand and speared the dog's mournful face. "Shut up, mutt!"

Beowulf cut his howl off in midstream and wagged his tail. "Chauvinist," Maeve muttered.

"Me?" Corbet asked gently.

"No. My dog," Maeve snapped. "There's something—can you hear?"

"I can hear," Corbet said. "Who couldn't? Between your dog and Packy Schultz, the whole settlement can hear."

"Packy? He's not here. Nobody's here, dammit!"

The singer, wherever he was, gave a couple of shouts. Maeve fell backward, into Ash's arms, her shiver of fear stamped down by the warmth of him. Until she looked down at his two hands. One of them held the bull's-eye lantern, solidly focused on the corner; the other held a very large, very frightening baseball bat!

"Oh, God," she muttered. "Don't hit me!"

"Of course not, love." The bat disappeared into the shadows behind him. "I wouldn't think of hitting you. But if there's anyone else... Now, work up a little courage, and walk over to your dog and pull him out of the corner. Got it?"

"I——"

"Come on, Mae. All it takes is a little courage," he coaxed.

"Yes. That's what I've got," she half whispered. "A little courage. A very little courage!"

"Hey. *My* girl always has a little courage left over." He gave her a little push. "Now, go over there and prove it!"

"Yes . . ." she muttered as her leaden legs carried her in the right direction. "Beowulf!"

"Whispering won't do it," he called to her. "Louder."

"BEOWULF!" Her dog gave her a lazy look, then, under urging, walked out of the corner to the door behind Ash. "I did it," she muttered.

"So you did. Now, if you ladies—oh, hi, Mrs. Wilson——"

"Hi, yourself," Carrie retorted.

At least one of us isn't frightened out of her wits, Maeve thought. And it isn't me!

"Now, if you ladies will step back a bit?" They did, while he came forward and knelt on the floor. "Mary, hold the lantern." It took both her hands to do so, but she made it.

"Here it is," he muttered. Maeve could see his finger toying with the projecting nail. He pushed it down. Nothing happened. He pulled it up. Nothing happened. "Damn!"

"Something wrong, Sherlock?"

"Don't be sarcastic. I hate sarcastic women. Ah, of course. Ladies, you're standing on the board."

"Well, of course we are," Maeve snapped. She had taken all she cared to from this arrogant man. "Did you want us to hang from the ceiling?"

"What I want," he said patiently, "is for the pair of you to step over there to one side."

An explanation in simple tones by a man who was fast losing his temper made it easier for Maeve to comply. She latched on to Carrie Wilson's arm and backed them both over to the other side of the room.

"And now, presto," Ash said. He pushed down on the nail. Nothing happened. He pulled up on the nail and there in the glare of the lantern an old rusted latch creaked and groaned, and a section of the floorboards in the shape of a trapdoor came up.

"My," Carrie said.

"My God," Maeve agreed.

Beowulf barked and grinned at them all, very proud of himself. A trapdoor, Maeve could see, that led to a cellar beneath the cement of the base of the house. A cellar lit now by a large lantern, similar to the one Ash was carrying. A lantern held by the shaky hand of Packy Schultz, from where he lay on the floor on a pile of burlap sacks and cardboard boxes with a big smile on his face.

"S'bout time," the old man grumbled. He waved a bottle in salute. An empty bottle of vodka. Another one lay at his feet, also empty. And surrounding him, row on row, were cases of other bottles, streaming away into the darkness.

"My own house," Maeve said in awe. "The only house in the settlement that has a cellar!"

"I don't believe it," Carrie said as she sidled closer to the opening. "All those rumors. I thought they were all a pipe dream!"

"An' I found 'em," Packy announced between hiccups. He managed to get to his feet, almost hitting his head on the beams, and executed a passable bow before he fell over on his face.

"I guess we'd better get the old coot out of there," Ash said. He wriggled around and dropped his legs into the pit. After considerable huffing and puffing he managed to get Packy's head and shoulders up to the floor level. "Well, pull," he said, exasperated.

"Pull? Yes, pull," Maeve agreed, her mind all awhirl. Packy Schultz and the lost treasure! She set the lantern down on the floor, took one of the old man's arms, and pulled. Packy Schultz had found the end of his rainbow!

The old man slid out onto the floor, clear of the trapdoor. Ash Corbet bent to look round the cellar, and then laughed as he vaulted easily out of the pit.

"Oh, Packy!" Maeve dropped to her knees and hugged her partner. "Oh, this is wonderful, Packy. But—why, you're crying."

"You will be, too," Packy said, enunciating carefully. "Why do you think I'm drinking vodka?"

"I—don't know," Maeve said, sighing. The man was drinking off a great celebration, and needed to be humoured. "I don't know. Why *are* you drinking vodka instead of all that marvellous old Rothschild 07?"

The old man staggered to his feet. Carrie was watching in rapture. Ash Corbet was laughing. "Because," Ash said funereally, "all the corks in those lovely wine bottles have been corroded, and probably that entire load has turned to vinegar!"

"Oh, shut up, you damn undertaker," Maeve roared. "That's not true, is it, Packy?"

"Gonna find me another bottle of vodka," that worthy said as he staggered out of the room, crying.

CHAPTER SEVEN

"THROW them out? You're out of your redheaded mind," Ash Corbet had told Maeve the night before. "First of all, not *all* the bottles *have* to be spoiled. I know a place south of here that could test every case. Do you know how much a bottle of this stuff is worth if it's good?" Maeve didn't, but swore to find out. "At worst, suppose it's all vinegar. Lady, that would be the finest vinegar in the world! Trust me. I'll get rid of it for you!"

And so a U-Haul truck had appeared that morning, and half the men in the settlement had laid down their various implements and had come to unload the cellar. "One case at a time, carefully," Maeve could hear Ash calling as she sat at her computer keyboard in the van.

"You know, this is all Chinese to me," Carrie Wilson said as she sat just behind Maeve and watched her fingers flying.

"Japanese," Maeve corrected her. "There are, all over the United States, central points where computer people maintain information for hackers—computer specialists. We call them Bulletin Boards, and to get one all I have to do is dial their telephone number. Now, the last one I called gave me a wine directory, and—here it is. Now, we just scan down the list until we come to Château Rothschild 07—Lord, Premier Grand Cru—one hundred and seventy-six dollars a bottle!"

Carrie whistled under her breath. "And you've got how many bottles?"

"Packy has," Maeve insisted. "Not me. About two thousand bottles. But he thinks they're all spoiled."

"Yes, but," said Carrie, the perpetual romantic, "suppose half of them are good?"

"I can't count that high," Maeve lied. If there was anything to be done with maths, she could do it, but had no wish to announce her skill to the world. Not with "Uncle Shamus" hanging around the edges of her life. "C'mon, we'd better make some edibles for the men."

"For *after* the job's done," Carrie insisted. "Feed them first and you'll lose your labor."

"I wish——" Maeve stopped for a moment as she parked the computer heads and shut the machine off. Something was misting in her right eye. She knuckled it out, whatever it was. She *needed* to talk to a woman. Get a sensible woman's viewpoint, instead of tying herself up in knots trying to live in a man's world!

"I wish I knew as much about the world as you do, Carrie. I really do. All of a sudden I realize my education is not complete. You know what I mean?"

"I know, dear. Care to tell me about it?"

"That's one of the problems. I don't understand *myself* well enough to tell it."

"So we'll guess," Carrie teased. "Is it smaller than a bread box or as big as a man?"

"You *know* it's a man," Maeve responded with some heat, and then giggled at herself. "Is that the way it is for a woman? Always a man?"

"Always. Some big, some little, but always male. So what's the problem?"

What's the problem? Maeve asked herself as she put her mind to it. "He's—a very nice man," she started out, fumbling around to get her thoughts in order. "Very nice." She mulled those words over. "He's good-looking,

in a—well, masculine sort of way." Another pause.
"He's friendly."

"Maybe more than friendly? Does he turn you on?"

"Like a damn electric light switch," Maeve confessed
moodily. "Whether I want to or not!"

"That's a step in the right direction," Carrie told her.
"So what's the trouble?"

"I—security," Maeve muttered, moving closer to the
other woman. "I have this hang-up about security. My
father died when I was young. I didn't have time for
being a child. We were always living on a roller coaster.
And now I've..."

Carrie let the long pause hang on the wind, and then
filled in the blank. "And now you've fallen in love?"

"I don't know, do I? Yes," Maeve countered in a rush,
finally willing to put the right words to it. "With a man
who has no visible means of support, who hangs around
doing as little as possible—and oh, Carrie, I think he's
mixed up with the underworld or something!"

The other woman leaned back in her chair, a frown
on her face. "How do you figure that?"

"Because—he has some kind of hold on people in
Cross City and Gainesville, and around here. I can't explain it, but every time he says a word or two somebody
jumps! Take this wine business. *He* knows a place that
can check it out; he also knows a place where he can
sell the stuff if it's turned to vinegar. Do *you* know places
like that? Does your *husband* know places like that?"

"No, I don't suppose Ralph does, dear."

"Gangsters do!"

"And all that makes you suspicious?"

"That and a lot of little things," Maeve said, sighing.
"No sooner do I think he's on the up-and-up than I
immediately smell things that tell me otherwise. I'm

going mad, Carrie. Stark raving mad! And now there's something big going on in the Cove. Smug——'' She strangled on the words. Telling Carrie might be like broadcasting to the world that smugglers were coming back to Smugglers Cove!

" 'Something big going on'?''

"I can't explain it, Carrie."

"I'm afraid I can't be much help, then," Carrie Wilson responded as she pushed her chair back and stood up. "I'm not a specialist in men, Mary. I only specialize in Ralph. Men aren't all alike, not by a darn sight. But I can tell you this. You'll never be happy with this man if you can't bring yourself to trust him. Marriage is built on trust." And with that little homily she swept out of the van and began doing noisy things in the kitchen.

And that, Maeve told herself, is what you get for wanderlust. If you had stayed home longer you'd have had your mother to talk to. But when you were home you were so wrapped up in computers that you never listened to Mother anyway. Should I telephone her? No, the telephone line is as leaky as a sieve. There's no way I can be sure that Ash Corbet or his friends aren't listening in to every conversation I start. Trust? How in God's world could I trust him? He ranks just under Uncle Shamus McCormac in the "Let's trust the dear man" department. Lawyering is an honorable trade; he doesn't seem to be very good at it. What in the name of heaven am I going to do? Love him or fight him? Or both? Carrie had just said you should never marry a man hoping to reform him. That never works. I'd better—I don't know what I'd better do, do I?

A cold muzzle thrust itself into her dangling hand. At least Beowulf would stand by her, she told herself as she forced herself up out of her chair and headed for the kitchen to help feed the workers.

The truck left at about ten in the morning, going gently with Ash Corbet in charge, and three volunteers to aid in the unloading. The others ate well. Maeve's call on the general store for cold cuts and bread had run that emporium out of almost everything on its shelves. Mounds of sandwiches had been made and displayed and devoured, and all the men—and the women too— had scattered. Maeve watched them go and waved from the back porch. Beowulf, strangely mute, sat at her side, his tail wagging.

"Well, just you and me," Maeve murmured to her dog as her hand ran in and out behind his ears. The excitement, and her talk with Carrie, had been a highlight; now she was on the other side of life, down in the dumps. Another light rain had moved in on the Cove. Not a driving storm wind, but rather a gentle downpour. The clouds were low and gray, the houses were higgledy-piggledy gray, her dog was elderly gray. "And so am I," she muttered. "So am I."

She walked back into the kitchen. The women had given the place a quick cleanup, but there was still a mess. She went over to the living-room door. The secret hatch was still open, and the room was buried in footprints and sand. There was one improvement. The front door, which had been stuck shut ever since her arrival in the Cove, had been the shortest route to the truck. A couple of the men had been eager to smash it open; instead, Ash had walked around to its outside and applied pressure over the pinewood panel with both hands. The hinges had creaked, the door groaned, and it opened, accompanied by a round of applause from the spectators. Ash had bowed and grinned straight at Maeve. She had felt the phantom kiss that had floated across to her over the heads of the crowd.

Maeve had watched every minute of the performance. He'd seemed so effortless, so powerful, and yet so gracefully agile. It reminded her of his "magic" act at the Saturday night dance. Sleight of hand? Or was it truly magic? She was almost ready to believe the latter, despite her scientific training. Almost. Maeve shrugged her shoulders, wished mightily that he had stayed behind after the truck left, and then got out broom and mop and dustpan, and set to work.

By two that afternoon, her house polished to a nicety, Maeve had made lunch for herself and Beowulf, showered, and wandered back to the van. The rain was still making Florida dismal, probably beyond the limits allowed by the State Constitution. She was smiling as she picked up the telephone. A word or two from her very sensible mother would certainly be useful.

The telephone crackled at her. The dial tone was present, but weak. It hardly made sense to dial long distance under those conditions. She was about to replace the receiver when a strong series of tones impinged on her ear. She knew automatically what it was. Someone in the local area was transmitting computer information on some or one of the lines within the wet local cable. Her hand flashed to the switches as she set her own machine to listen and record. Her computer hummed at her, gurgled, processed, and presented an unreadable pattern on her screen. Of course, she told herself. Encoded!

The word was like a dare. As with any computer "freak," Maeve was highly curious. Any code could be broken. In fact, in her lexicon, codes were *made* to be broken. How else could she get a good night's sleep? The Twelfth Commandment, to Maeve McCormac and her computer peers, was, "Thou Shalt Not Suffer an Encoded Message to Escape Untranslated!"

The first step, as always, was to answer the question: "What program was that unidentified computer using?" Within her files Maeve had samples from practically every commercial computer program in the country. Now she set the switches and commanded her own machine to begin a comparison check. It might take a great deal of the machine's time, but that was what computers did best. All the grimy little details that a human mind abhorred. With a grim little smile on her face she pushed the "Search" key and sat back to wait.

The wait ran through the afternoon and into the evening, through the rain storm and into the star pattern of a clear warm night. And then there were noises at her front door, and Beowulf barked a greeting.

Maeve slipped out of her contour chair in front of her computer screen, and ran for the door. "Now that," Ash Corbet said from outside the locked screen, "is what I call a decent welcome." Her fingers fumbled with the latch, and he brushed past her to kneel and pat her dog.

"I thought you meant me," Maeve grumbled pettishly. The time of doubting had fled as her eyes feasted on him. He came up from one knee and grinned at her.

"I *did* mean you," he said, chuckling. Those long arms surrounded her, held her close, the softness of her rounded cheek pressed against the rough texture of his shirt. Remember what you were thinking this afternoon, her inner self tried to warn, but Maeve had already forgotten. Only the warmth of him filled her, only the masculine smell of him impinged on her nostrils, only the dream of him became a reality. Independent little

Maeve McCormac surrendered herself, body and soul, and strained up hard against him, from knee to shoulder to heart.

It might have been years later that they stirred. "I came over——" he started to say, and then stopped. Came over to what? Maeve thought. To stand and hold me all night? To see if two could really sleep in my bed? To touch——?

"To ask you to come out fishing with me again," he said, interrupting her more erotic thoughts.

"To what?" She pushed away from him, barely clearing an inch or two against his confining arms, and stared indignantly up at him.

"Fishing," he repeated. "You know, as in hook and line, and boat, and things like that?"

"You must be out of your ever-loving mind," she sputtered. "Nobody goes fishing at night. Nobody!"

"Not true," he assured her solemnly. "What could be better? The Gulf is as smooth as a baby's—er—bottom. All the little fish will be nesting for the night. We can lie back and count the stars."

"Fish don't nest," she snapped, but he had already sold the story, and seemed to know she was weakening.

"So they'll be doing whatever it is they do without bothering us," he said softly, his lips close to her ear. And after a moment's silence, "Maeve?"

"Yes," she said, sighing. "Why not?"

His arms tightened, pulled her back against him, hugged her gently. She could feel the light touch as his lips brushed against her hair. A little shiver of delight flashed up and down her spine. Together, arm in arm, they strolled out of the door sideways, laughing to see who might go first. Beowulf moaned an appeal.

"Stay," Maeve commanded. "Guard."

"What's to guard?"

"I have a program running on my computer."

"And your dog knows to shut it off if it gets in trouble?"

"No," Maeve told him. "But he *thinks* he does. And, besides, if he comes along with us——"

"He'll be like a bloody chaperon," Ash interrupted. "I don't need that."

And neither do I, Maeve told herself, but I'm darned if I'll tell *him* that!

His boat was nowhere near the magnitude of Rob Stanley's. About twenty-five feet long, with an open cockpit and a tiny windshield to protect the helmsman, it was powered by a pair of powerful outboard motors— and it swung at anchor almost twenty yards offshore. Maeve searched up and down the beach in the gathering darkness.

"I don't see a dinghy," she said hesitantly.

"No. I can't afford one of those," he returned.

"Then how do we get out to the boat?"

"Easy. We swim," he replied. "You *do* swim?"

"I swim," she answered, "but I didn't bring a swimsuit with me."

"Why, I thought everyone was born with one," he commented. It was too dark for her to see the teasing look in his eyes. "I'm wearing mine."

"Well, if you think what I think you think," she snapped, "forget it! Surely you don't expect me to—you *do* expect me to, don't you?"

"Now, fireball, don't put words in my mouth. That's a lovely pair of shorts you're wearing, and a lovely halter.

The water is warm, the night air is warm. All we have
to do is wade in and swim out. Simple."

Maeve had to think that one over for a moment. Her
stop-and-go mind hadn't considered all the implications
of a moonlight spin, not by a darn sight. What he said
seemed eminently practical. But how was he to know
that the shorts and halter were *all* she was wearing at
the moment? "I could go back and get my suit," she
muttered.

"Waste of time," he assured her. "Ready?"

She wasn't, but dealing with Ash Corbet was like riding
some juggernaut. There seemed to be nowhere to say,
"No," and nowhere to get off! So her mind sputtered
for a moment, the same moment that he employed to
tug her by the hand out into the cool water, and by the
time she had decided what to say it was too late.

He swam like a fish, idling along beside her with easy
strokes. Maeve was a journeyman swimmer. She
measured her goal and plugged seriously ahead with
short choppy movements, hoping that her strength would
exceed her limitations. He made it look so easy that she
could feel her temper rising, and might have managed
a word or two had not her hand slapped against the side
of the boat.

"Up you go," he caroled in her ear. The hand at her
waist shifted lower, cupped her pert posterior, and almost
threw her up and over the rail. In another second he
came splashing up and over the side, like a hungry shark
looking for dinner.

"You don't have to land on top of me," she muttered.
"It's a big boat, after all."

"Clumsiness," he returned as he rolled over and away
from her. "You can take the boy out of the country, but
you can't take the country out of the boy."

"Horsefeathers!" Maeve struggled to her feet and wrapped herself up in her own arms. Her tiny bits of clothing clung to her like a second skin. A small wind was blowing in off the Gulf. As it set about evaporating the water in her apparel it left her chilled, even though the night was warm. So chilled that her teeth chattered.

"Hey, perhaps this wasn't the best idea I ever had," he said as he came up to her and hugged her. His own shirt and shorts were as wet as hers, and there was no comfort to be found. She felt as miserable as she had the day her father had died, and bitterness set in.

"If you were a gentleman you would have swum out by yourself," she snapped, "and brought the boat in close enough for me to wade to it."

"If I were a gentleman and brought the boat in another six feet it would still be aground," he told her bleakly. "I suppose you don't care to fish now?"

"You suppose ever so rightly," she told him, and her whole body shivered. "You could even have brought your boat in at my dock and picked me up, and I'd be dry as a bone."

"I didn't even think about that," he admitted.

"Rob Stanley would have."

"God, you really know how to stab a guy in the gut, don't you?" he muttered. "Well, we're here and you're cold. At least we can do something about that. I have a blanket here somewhere. You slide out of your shorts and halter, and we'll wrap you in a blanket."

"*We'll* do nothing of the sort."

"Come on, Mary Kennedy. I'm sure your underwear is as formidable as your chin at this moment."

"I'm sure it is," she replied. And it's all lying on my bed back at the cottage! No, you don't catch me that easily, Ash Corbet. I'm not going to stand around here in the altogether while you wrap me up in an old blanket!

"What the devil have I come up with?" he grumbled. "A Puritan? Well, here, slip the blanket around you and you'll be free from my lusting eyes."

Maeve hesitated. It was as dark as the inside of a bowl with the lid on, and only a few bright stars penetrated the gloom. The warmth of the blanket on her shoulders was delightful. Ash was standing at the bow of the boat, as far from her as he could get without falling overboard. And besides, she told herself, you're *not* a Puritan. You came along because you wanted—what?

Her mind was not about to admit just what she wanted from him. Her jump out of childhood into the adult world had brought with her a whole basket of restraints and judgments and moralities. None of that had bothered her at all, not until she'd met Ash Corbet, and now her stern little world was being shaken down to its lowest morality. "Get a grip on yourself," she muttered as she dropped the blanket and hastily shed her wet shorts and halter. They fell in a damp clump around her ankles, and when she tried to kick them away she stumbled and almost fell.

He wasn't as far away as she had thought. As she wavered, one of his strong hands caught her left arm to steady her. The other reached out blindly, and landed on her right breast. The shock of the gentle contact immobilized her. His hand jumped away as if he too had felt the shock and could not bear the fire of it. But she was still rocking on her feet, and the missing hand came back, somewhat lower, and managed to lock on to her bare right hip.

"Great day in the morning," he muttered. "Isn't there any place that's—?"

"No," she said. "No place." His lower hand patted her right flank gently, and he stooped away from her and came up with the blanket. Ash wrapped it around her shoulders at what seemed to her to be an unconscionably slow speed. A turtle could have done better.

The blanket brought instant warmth, but Maeve regretted losing the contact with his hand, and she whimpered a little protest.

"Something else wrong?" he asked.

"No, I—nothing." He sighed as he pulled her blanket-draped form against his own. Her hands went out to him. His skin was still dripping wet. Her hand wandered. He was all skin, all the way down to his——

"Don't you have another blanket?" she asked plaintively. Her mind was telling her hand to move away; her body was having none of that. The hand stayed where it was.

"No," he said, chuckling, "but a couple more minutes of this and I won't need one, will I?"

"Oh, you!" She snatched her hand away indignantly. Blood pounded into her cheeks. Maeve was glad for the protection of the darkness. Blushing was a trait that a woman her age should have long since outgrown. She moved away from him, found a bench pressing at the back of her knees, and collapsed on to it. Her mind was in conflict with itself. One half said, "Tell him to take me home." The other half said, "Tell him to take me." And there was no way Maeve McCormac could come to a choice between the two.

He did it for her. She could feel the boat rock as he moved toward the bow and pressed the starter button. The huge outboard motor burst into chatter, sputtered, then smoothed itself out. After the first outburst of noise the machine became very quiet. She could see his darker shadow as he cast off from the anchor buoy, and the boat began to move slowly away from the shore. Maeve looked behind her, to where the lights of the settlement marked the anchorage. A strange thought flooded her mind. Behind her was the settled life, the marriage to her computers, the world she had always known. Ahead of her was the open Gulf, and a path unknown.

Ash Corbet did something complicated at the control panel, and then padded back to sit beside her. Maeve moved an inch or two away from him, instantly regretted it, and came back until her hip was hard up against his. "No running lights?" she asked cautiously.

"They'd scare the fish," he told her solemnly.

"But—it's against the law to ride with no running lights. Someone might hit us."

"That's all I need," he sighed as his arm came around her shoulder. "A Puritan sea lawyer."

"I—are you disgusted with me?" she asked. There was a little tremolo in her voice. His big hand gripped her shoulder and squeezed gently.

"No. Never. Are you disgusted with me?"

"No. I knew when I agreed to come."

"Knew what?"

"That's the trouble," she replied. "I can't remember what I knew. You're cold!"

"You wouldn't know that if you kept your hands inside your blanket," he admonished. "Didn't your mother ever tell you anything?"

"Yes, but I never listened. What girl does? I thought I knew it all. Why don't you——?" A moment of silence, penetrated only by the gentle hum of the motor as they barely maintained headway.

"Why don't I what?"

"This is a very big blanket. Why don't you come inside with me?" Whispered, because she lacked the courage to commit herself, and then repeated firmly as she opened one side of the blanket and tried to push it around his shoulders.

"You really mean that, Maeve?"

Of course I do, you big clumsy ox, she thought. But I'll never tell you. Never. Why couldn't I have fallen in love with a nice young man in Apalachicola? Why am I sitting in a cold boat with a warm man, waiting for him to do whatever he's going to do? Why doesn't he hurry? Why is it that a woman always has to wait for the man to initiate—whatever? If I knew what to do, I'd do it!

Not knowing; that was her cue. She had heard a great deal of talk in school, seen more than a few "R"-rated movies, and still she didn't quite know how it was done. So she angrily pushed the end of the blanket at him, and finally he took charge, wrapping the heavy material until it covered them both. And left them body to body, sharing the warmth of each other. Maeve shivered again. Not from the cold, but rather from the anticipation.

His arm came around her back, the hand touching her just under her breast. Another shiver racked her body. "Don't worry, little Mae," he murmured in her ear. "Nothing's going to happen that you don't want."

"But that's the trouble," she complained in a little-girl voice. "I don't know what I want. Could we just—talk?"

"Why not?" He was laughing at her. She could hear it in his voice as his chin rested in the middle of her wet curls. "So talk."

"I—don't know what to say."

"So tell me how little... Mary Kennedy... got to be what she is?"

That little pause just before her adopted name gave Maeve another little shiver, which passed quickly away. There was no way Ash Corbet could know who she really was. No way. And besides it was warm here in their little cocoon. She squirmed a little closer, resting her back in the middle of his chest. His hand moved up the hill of her breast and treasured it. The delicious feeling spread throughout her body and into her mind. This is the way it's supposed to be, she told herself, if you love the man. She squirmed a little closer. And if he loves you, her inner self told her. That last was more of a question than a statement, and Maeve McCormac did not know the answer. She squirmed a little further, and managed to look up into his face. And could see nothing, so she turned back to her original resting place and pondered what to tell him.

One of his hands was holding the blanket. Both of hers were free. A small movement of his finger and thumb at her nipple brought a gasp from Maeve. There was no way she could talk while all this was going on. She brought both her hands up over his and clamped it in place. He chuckled again and kissed her forehead gently.

"I—was a perfectly normal little girl," she said, sighing. "Until my father died. My mother is handicapped. Limited to a wheelchair. So somewhere between my sixth and seventh birthday I became the mistress of the house. Stop that!" His wiggling thumb ceased.

"You don't like that?"

"I—it doesn't matter whether I like it or not," she answered firmly. "I just can't... think... when you do that. And I need to think."

"So you became mistress of the house," he prompted.

"Yes. There was always so much to do. Dad left us pretty well fixed, but everything had to be managed, you know. When I was nine I bought my first computer. Fell in love with it, so to speak. And spent the next few years managing and studying computing, and going to university, and——"

"And what?"

"I don't know," she half whispered. "Now that I look back on it all it just seems that I was so involved with my work that I lost touch with people. Even my mother. Oh, I saw that she was comfortable, and spent time with her in between my travels, but it was almost as if she had become a shadow among all the other shadows I worked with, and only I was the real person. Does that make sense?"

"And something woke you up?"

"Just recently," she told him. "The Cove, the activities here, Carrie, and—and you. It stirred my stomach. Made me realize how much of life I've been missing. I've been arguing with myself for the past week or so."

"And you've come down on the side of change, Mae? I'm glad. You *are* my girl, you know." She fumbled with one hand and found his bare knee under the blanket. A gentle pat, and then she left it there at rest.

"I don't know," she answered him. "I just don't know if I want to be *anybody's* girl."

"What you need to do is to tell me the *whole* truth," he said suddenly. "And then you'll know."

"Do you say so?" He turned her whole body until she lay across his lap, still in his arms, still covered by the blanket. "Wouldn't it be a surprise if we *both* were to tell the whole truth, Ash?"

"Are you suggesting that I'm not telling you the whole truth?" Again that demon laugh was behind his words.

"I..." She was about to lay him out in lavender. He was telling her so little of the truth that he ought to be registered as a member of Congress. But what she planned to do, what she was angry enough to do, hardly mattered. He lifted her up and bent down at the same time, and somewhere between love and high tide his lips met hers and shut off all the words.

Some minutes later, when she managed to catch a breath, she asked dreamily, "Do you think that kissing will change anything?"

"Yes. Everything," he insisted as he stood up, still holding her in his arms. The blanket dropped off into the scuppers, but they were dry now, and the wind was no longer serving as a refrigerator. He bent over, and Maeve could feel the coolness of the wooden deck against her back as he rescued the blanket and tucked it under her.

"This doesn't look like kissing." She was shivering again, in anticipation. Whatever it looked like, she meant to lie back and enjoy it. He *had* to love her, or he wouldn't do all this. And she *had* to love him, or she would never allow it. "Are you trying to seduce me, Ash Corbet?"

"I believe I am, ma'am." He was hovering over her now on hands and knees, facing the bow. She reached up to pull him down against her aching breasts. Another kiss, this time with his body length against hers, his weight coming down between her thighs, his hands roaming up and down her soft tender frame. And then he paused.

"Good God, don't stop now," she moaned hoarsely.

"Hush," he commanded as he levered his body back up and moved up in the cockpit. In a moment the sound of their outboard motor trailed away. From somewhere off in the port quarter she could hear the steady slow thumping of a diesel engine.

Maeve scrambled to her knees, clutching at the rail, straining her eyes. She could barely perceive Ash's outline as he drew a pair of binoculars out of the cuddy by the wheel. Long heavy binoculars—expensive night-vision binoculars.

"Damn," he muttered. "Are they early or is this a practice run?"

"How would I know?" she spat angrily. "This is really what you wanted to come out here for, wasn't it? To check up on——?"

"Shut up," he commanded in an undertone. Maeve stuck her tongue out at him, recovered the blanket, and retreated to the stern, where an upholstered bench offered comfort. How about that? she told herself bitterly. He's out here on some smuggling mission, and brought me along just to—to pass the time of night! Damn the man! And that will be the last "please" and "thank you" he'll ever get from me!

For some minutes, as the sound of the other boat increased and then faded away, Maeve sat there, letting her temper rise to white heat, while Ash leaned against the control panels, his binoculars following the other boat. Finally Ash put the glasses away and walked back the length of the boat to her side.

"Another boat without running lights," she commented in a brittle voice. "It seems to be a habit around here."

"Yes, it does," he admitted as he slouched down beside her, consulting his wristwatch. "Now, where were we?"

"Oh? You've got time between appointments for me?" There was enough acid in her tone to kill all the fish in the Gulf of Mexico.

"Don't be like that, Mae." His hand reached around her; she carefully lifted it and returned it to him.

"You were enjoying it all," he coaxed. She glared at him in the dark, wishing it wouldn't be unladylike to bite him.

"Well, I've been made a fool of many times in my young life," she answered bitterly, "but managed to recover."

"Mae——"

"Take me home, Mr. Corbet," she interrupted him as she moved as far away from him as the boat would allow.

"Mae?"

"Take me home." In the darkness she could not see him as he stared in her direction, then shrugged his shoulders. He was muttering under his breath as he pushed the starter button and headed them back toward Smugglers Cove.

CHAPTER EIGHT

SATURDAY morning, early, Maeve McCormac sat on the jumble of rocks, all that was left of her sea wall, and stared out to sea with blurred eyes. Beowulf, upset by her attitude, lay at her feet, whining from time to time.

"It's okay, boy," she said to comfort the old dog, but her voice displayed her lassitude, her own doubts. Her weary hand fondled the ruff of fur on Beowulf's neck, but it was not the same. Not to her, not to her dog. Her whole world had changed in one night, and not for the better.

Ash Corbet had brought her home to her own dock late the previous night. Once or twice he'd looked as if he was going to say something and then changed his mind. So, clad in her still-damp shorts and halter, she had climbed to the dock, turned back a moment to look down at him in the cockpit of his boat, and then strode away without saying a word herself.

Maeve had tossed and turned all night, unable to sleep, unwilling to get up to do something useful. And, when the morning sun had come up over the Suwannee swamps behind the house, she had dressed in her most ragged jeans, gray blouse, gray sandals, and had come down to the soothing sounds of the waves to wrestle with her conscience.

Back home she might have plucked a wildflower and pulled its petals off one at a time, quoting the old saying, "He loves me, he loves me not." This part of Florida was not overloaded with wildflowers, and, besides, she didn't need to guess. He loves me not. Certainly a woman could not ask for more proof? He had gone into the night looking for—expecting—another boat to be at sea. And he had taken her along as a convenience. A one-night boating adventure.

He hadn't got what he'd wanted, and in some perverse way she was glad for that. She hadn't lost her virtue. And that wild thought brought a grimace to her pretty face. Twice she had almost "lost her virtue." Last night, and once years ago. Both times, she reminded herself, she had been eager to give it away, not to "lose" it. The first time, in the back seat of an old Oldsmobile, trying to keep up with her peers, she had almost succeeded—with the most handsome boy in her school. She had loved him madly, that boy whose name she couldn't even remember now. But the police had been patrolling Lovers' Lane that night, and in his wild excitement her partner had inadvertently pushed the door open and Maeve had slid off the seat, falling out of the car on the opposite side from the police cruiser, leaving the young man to explain it all to the Law. And now, having offered everything to Ash Corbet, she had been snubbed by his interest in another *boat*, for goodness' sakes! How could a grown woman work against *that* sort of competition?

Dolefully Maeve got up, brushed down her jeans, and started back up to the house. "Come on, pup. I'll make a big breakfast for you to eat." Beowulf, whose vocabulary consisted of six words, three of which were eat, struggled to his feet and tagged along after her. Ash Corbet was leaning indolently against the post of her back porch.

"Is there something you wanted, Deputy?" Her fingers curled into claws, the nails sharp and ready. There was nothing she wouldn't be willing to do to this man. For this man? Her confused mind struggled with the implication of her thoughts.

He shook his head from side to side, as if trying to parry a blow. "I thought I'd come down and apologize for last night," he said. But Maeve was giving no ground.

"Are you really?" she asked in a high tense voice. "Sorry, that is?"

"Yes." He looked down at her for a moment. "Well, to be truthful, no. I enjoyed every bit of it, up until the last minute or two."

"Too bad," she snapped at him. "The fish got away. And I wish you would do the same."

"Ah, sweet Mae," he said, sighing. "You wouldn't hold one little mistake against a man?"

"That shows how little you know me," she said firmly. "Yes, I would. Now, I'm sure you have some big business deal to transact—somewhere else. No?"

"As it happens, I do," he told her. "I have to run up to—er—the north. But when I get back tonight we'll have a talk, you and I."

"Damned if we will," she muttered. Either he didn't hear the comment, or he was ignoring her in his usual brash way, because he shook his head again, then pushed off from the porch and walked up the path, whistling. "He'll never get that right," Maeve told her dog. "He can't whistle worth a hill of beans."

Some hours later she finished feeding her dog. Just Beowulf, not herself. Her own needs were satisfied by a mug of coffee. Anger gave her enough incentive to wield the broom, dust the most obvious places, and make her bed. Anger and loneliness. Ash Corbet was already out of her mind—but evidently her mind was not prepared to accept this new scheme of things. Neither was Beowulf, who must be taught just who her enemies were if he was to guard her and her household. So she sat down at lunchtime and lectured her animal, to no apparent effect.

Late in the afternoon, after a long walk up the beach and back, she wandered out into the van, and stopped in astonishment. The floor was flooded with reams of paper; the machine was sitting there blinking in a very self-satisfied rhythm. Her computer had solved the problem she had set for it—set and forgotten.

Her first impulse was to gather up all that paper and make a bonfire out of it. Her second was the cautious acknowledgment that she really wanted to know what the solution was. She pushed the mass of paper to one side, clearing a way to her chair, and then tore off the last sheet in the printer. All the rest, she quickly realized, were records of how the computer had arrived at its conclusions, and were unnecessary.

The machine had reduced its problem to three choices, all equally possible, and printed those choices out for human evaluation. Maeve closed her eyes for a moment. A, B, or C. Random choice. Her finger slammed down on the "B" key. Her machine began to spew out a half-page of sheer gibberish. Not B at all. So, C? She tapped gently on the keyboard, the machine gurgled at her, and began to print in English. Her eyes followed the words as they appeared.

"Saturday, 18 June. Land 2300. Unload 0100, cross swamp by pirogue. Arrive highway 0600. Have truck meet. Acknowledge."

"So, it's all true," Maeve muttered. "Smuggling!" Her heart fell down into her boots. Smuggling something. The only place they could land a load was at her dock. Whatever it was they were smuggling had to fit into one of the long narrow boats, pirogues, that could be poled across the swamp. And a truck to meet them at some convenient spot on the highway. So, if the smugglers were to be stopped, something had to happen here at her dock, or in the few hundred yards of dry land that was Smugglers Cove. Once they were into the swamp no one would be able to find them, no dog would be able to track them.

It had never crossed Maeve's mind that she should not be part of that "stopping" crew. She knew the plan. She and—whoever else had sent the message? And it was at that point that her mind slammed into a blank wall. She and Packy had searched every cottage in the Cove. There were only two houses which contained computer equipment. Her own, and Ash Corbet's!

"Oh, God," she muttered. She tried to relax, her head at rest on the high back of her chair. But it was an ineffective try. Ash Corbet. How many times in the past few weeks had she thought of him as the bad guy? How many times had she fought that conclusion, because she loved him? And now she had found the "smoking gun." Logic could sustain only one conclusion, and, although her heart cried at the thought, she had to take some action against the man she still loved. Yes, even after last night, she still loved him.

So the next question then became, "What action?" Maeve sprang up from her chair, went out into the house, and paced the tiny rooms. Beowulf, feeling her need, whined and crouched in a corner. Ten paces forward, eight to the right, ten back—what to do? What can you say, who can you appeal to, when the law itself is the lawbreaker? There were no other men in the Cove she could turn to—no one, that was, but Rob Stanley. And even with him she had doubts. What was it that Ash had called him? A "small-time developer"? Hardly the sort of man to appeal to in an emergency.

Nervously, shaking, she checked her watch. Four in the afternoon already, and the unloading was scheduled for 2300 hours. Eleven o'clock that night, expressed in International time. Perhaps—if she just warned Ash that she knew? He might possibly back out, giving her time to... to do *something* else. Not a brilliant idea, but the only one that came to mind.

Maeve rushed back into the computer room and folded all the mass of paper into a neat package containing the whole story. Shake the evidence in his face, she told herself grimly. See if the "poor country boy" could be bluffed into changing his plans.

"Guard, Beowulf," she commanded, and slammed out of the back door, running. No house in the Cove was particularly far from any other, but Ash's was the furthest from her own, up at the north end of the settlement. A couple of people, including Carrie Wilson, called to her as she hurried by. Maeve barely acknowledged them, and ran on.

Packy Schultz was standing at the front door of Corbet's house when she came up to him, almost completely out of breath.

"In trainin' or somethin'?" The old man looked a decade younger than he had before they had found the wine cache. "Hey, hold on, little lady. Ain't no sense to run yourself to death."

"Is Ash—is Mr. Corbet at home?" she gasped.

"Nope. Done gone off somewheres," Packy told her. "You ain't heard yet about the wine?"

"No." Maeve collapsed on the front steps of the porch to catch her breath. "No, not a word. Would think it might take some time. I have to talk to Mr. Corbet. I *have* to."

"Be more'n obliged to find him, but I ain't got no idea where to look," the old man said. "Went off in that big car of his, along with a couple of strangers. Was you lookin' for the mayor, the deputy sheriff, or the lawyer? If I knew which one of him you wanted it might help." The old man managed a dry rasping cackle at his little joke.

"I—think I need the sheriff," Maeve decided.

"Then you best git over to the County Court House," Packy told her. "Don't know no place else you can get that kind of help. Cross City, that is. You know the way."

"I know the way," Maeve told him, still almost out of breath. She consulted her watch again. Time was running out, but she needed a second string to her bow, just in case. "Packy, could you do me a favor?"

"For you, partner? Anything."

"I'm going to Cross City," she said. "If things don't work out right I'll come directly back, and in that case I could use some male help. Do you suppose you could stay over at my house until I get back, just in case?"

"Suppose I could," he assured her. "Freebies in the refrigerator?"

"Anything you want. Help yourself."

Before he could wedge in another word Maeve was back on her feet, running in the reverse direction, heading for her little car and the long ride across the swamp road to Dixie County seat. She drove at full speed, with the windows open. It was probably the draughts and the wind that filled her eyes with tears. Or so she told herself.

* * *

Nine o'clock, on a moonless Florida night. Cross City had almost closed down; all but the County Court House. Dixie County was small, and the business of the county attorney was small crimes, but in the height of the summer there were a very large number of them. The lights were still bright in the tiny office, and the big man behind the desk was tired. He reserved one day a week for paperwork. One long day, and this was it. But now his desk was clean. He settled back in his wooden swivel chair, the same one his father had used as a judge on the Circuit Court, and placed one scuffed shoe on the clear desk top. The door opened and his part-time secretary came in.

"I've got this all cleared out, Mabel," he said. "Wish I had a cigar."

"You gave up smoking a year ago," the motherly secretary told him. "And twice the year before."

"Now, come on, Mabel," he said, laughing. "It's not that I lack *willpower*, it's just that I lack *won't* power. What've you got there?"

"Another one of those crank things," Mabel said. "I didn't want to bother you with it, but she was desperate so I promised I'd lay the file on the county attorney's desk."

"Seems as if there are more crackpots in the county every year," he agreed. "But I think I'd better head for home. What's the little lady's problem?"

"I'm not really sure that I know. She claimed to be a computer expert who had tapped on to a strange message down in the Cove——"

The county attorney's foot came down off the desk, and his chair slammed forward. "Down at the Cove? A computer expert? Dear God! What did she say?"

"She said she had decoded a computer message being sent out of the Cove, having to do with a smuggling shipment coming in tonight. She said it was all here in these computer sheets, but I can't read head nor tails of them."

"My God," he repeated. "As simple as that? We've been snooping around the Cove for months, not picking up a thing, and just like that she—don't tell me. Her name was not Mary Kennedy?"

"Okay, so I won't tell you," Mabel told him with a straight face, "but, yes, it was Mary Kennedy."

He was fumbling through the papers as his secretary poked fun at him. "Tonight," he muttered. "Twenty-three hundred hours. And that crazy woman is probably running off to stop them single-handed! Listen here, what exactly did she say?"

"Well, she asked to see the county attorney. I told her you were too busy, but if she wanted to wait until eight o'clock I might work her in."

"And?"

"So she paced up and down the outer office until seven o'clock, and then she muttered something about how she couldn't wait any longer, and dumped this stack of paper on my desk and vanished."

"Dear God," he muttered as he thumbed through the papers. "You should have brought her in the minute she arrived, Mabel. Did she know who was *sending* the message?"

"Well, that's why I didn't bring her in," his secretary told him, smiling. "She said she knew all right. She said it was Ash Corbet!"

"Oh, brother," Ash Corbet moaned as he reached for the telephone. "What the devil is that number for the State Police Emergency Reaction squad?"

* * *

Maeve McCormac slammed back down the narrow stairs and out of the building, disgusted with officialdom. Her watch said seven-fifteen, and the sun was low in the west, shining through a haze of red dust. Four hours before the landing—of whatever it was they were landing. Four hours. She put her foot to the floor and the car jumped. Luckily there was no traffic on highway three-fifty-one. If there had been the other drivers would have been scared out of their wits. She managed the twenty miles or more at a mile-a-minute speed, the little car wavering and skidding on the twists and turns of the road.

Packy was waiting for her, faithfully. The old man had successfully guarded the bakery lemon-meringue pie. Some of the frosting was still on his upper lip. Beowulf had faithfully guarded the shoulder of fresh ham she had left in the refrigerator. The bone was all that was left, and the corner of the kitchen floor was greasy. Neither of them were gourmet eaters.

"All right, you guys," she said as she collapsed onto a kitchen chair. "Listen up." Her explanation of the problem was intriguing. Packy even stopped licking his fingers.

"So, we go down to the dock just before time," the old man suggested, "and we put the snatch on whatever they're carryin'."

"We what?"

"We hijack their load. This had better be some sassy scam. I don't got a gun to my name, an'' smugglers usually carry a piece or two. You—you don't have no gun? I'd think a smart kid like you would be packing an arsenal. No?"

"No." Maeve shook her head. Those bronze curls swayed across her face and back. But I *wish* I weren't so scared of the darn things, she told herself. I wish...

Maybe the sheriff will ride up on his white horse and—oh, hell! "I think," Maeve said slowly, shocked back to reality, "that maybe we need more help."

"Only man in the settlement besides Ash Corbet with any guts is that Wilson feller," Packy announced. "The rest of them is losers from the word go."

"I'm afraid you're right," Maeve sighed. "And Ralph is away at Disney World with all his kids."

Packy shrugged his shoulders.

"But," Maeve mused, "we could always go over to Watch Hill and get Rob Stanley."

"Don't know a single good thing to say about *that* man," her partner declared. "Not a single thing."

"Well, *I* do. He's big. Come on, you two. I need every pair of hands—and teeth——" that said apologetically to the dog "—that I can get."

Her troops followed her reluctantly. Out of the door, down to the beach, and around the corner of the hill, ploughing through sand too deep for her little car to manage. It was the first time that Maeve had seen the house from ground level.

"Oh, my," she muttered, wondering if her plan had come unstuck. But it was too late to turn back. Rob Stanley's house was a wood and brick structure fitted neatly into the contours of the hill. The front was more glass than anything else. The tower she had seen once before from above looked to be about five storeys high when seen from down on the beach. Light sparkled from every window. From somewhere in the distance she could hear an electric generator thumping. "Come on," she muttered, and started up the slate-paved walk to the front door.

"I need to see Mr. Stanley," she told the tall young man who answered the bell.

"He isn't seeing anyone tonight." He spoke with a guttural accent, but Florida is full of strangers, she told herself.

"Look, don't try to put me off. I've had enough of that at the county attorney's office," she snapped back at him. "There's something rotten going down here in the Cove, and I need Rob's help. Now!"

Something impressed the man. It might have been her imperious attitude, or the way she stamped her foot, or the motley crew behind her. In any event he stepped aside and motioned her into the house. "Wait in here—please." He gestured toward a sitting room on the right-hand side of the entrance corridor. The man sounded as if "please" and "thank you" were not his favorite words. "I'll tell Mr. Stanley."

"You do that," Maeve said firmly. There were over-stuffed lounge chairs scattered about the room. She sank into one of them with a massive sigh. It had been a long day. Her watch said eight forty-five.

"I don't know if I like this at all," Packy said. The old man was sitting on the edge of the chair across from Maeve, his feet planted on the red carpet as if he was ready for a running start to somewhere else. Beowulf refused to sit. He moved to the window area and paced back and forth, growling softly. Another man appeared at the door, took one quick look inside, and then established a sentry post there, watching from the corridor.

"It'll be all right," Maeve assured Packy, wishing she believed it herself. There was something sinister about this whole affair. Rob Stanley had more men around the place than Beowulf had fleas. Her hands twisted nervously in her lap and she squirmed around to watch that door.

It must have been a good half hour before Rob Stanley came in. Maeve took a quick check on her wristwatch. It was nine-thirty.

"Well, what a surprise," the big blond man said as he strode into the room. "A social call?" He walked over to Maeve's chair. Beowulf moved up on the other side of her and growled a warning. Stanley looked down at the dog, perplexed.

"Not exactly." Maeve looked at his broad open face, his bright blue eyes fixed on her. A saying of her mother's came to her: Watch out for the man who can look you straight in the eye: he's about to tell you the world's biggest lie. But there's no time to waffle, Maeve told herself, and no time to back out. "We have this difficulty, Rob," she said, and proceeded to tell him everything about the smuggling plot.

"Say, that *is* a problem," Stanley said in his most genial voice. "Smuggling? And using our—I mean, your dock? Have you tried to contact the authorities?"

"Nobody would listen," Maeve admitted ruefully. "You're my last hope. Will you help?"

"Very complicated," he hedged. "Very complicated."

"He'll help," another voice said from the doorway. Maeve craned her neck to see. It was the same short dapper moustached man she had seen through her binoculars that day on top of Watch Hill. There was a peculiar but exact accent to his English. She had heard that accent before. Upper-class English, but with some twist to it. Australian? Arab? South African?

Maeve turned back to Rob Stanley. His normally smooth face was mottled—in anger or in fear? Whatever the reason, the big man seemed to shrink, as if someone had let some of the air out of his balloon.

"No, Rolf," Rob said.

"Don't be a fool," Rolf said. "We need this setup for a permanent operation, not a hit-and-run affair. The syndicate has put a great deal of money into the development. There are so many people running drugs into Florida that we must find some unusual way to bring in our diamonds. And now she knows all about it. You're lucky, Stanley, that she hasn't gone to the police. When the shipment goes, she goes with it."

"But that's——"

"Purely a business proposition," Rolf interrupted. "Purely business. Tie them up and let's get down to the dock."

Maeve struggled to find her courage. Only a fool could not interpret the threat. They might all start out on this journey, but she and Packy would only be going halfway! A quick glance across at the old man told her that he knew. There was a bleak wariness about his face, a desperate awareness.

"Tie them up," Rolf repeated, and two more men came in from the hall. The shorter one went directly to Maeve, reached down and pulled her up out of her chair roughly. He had barely completed his move when he was struck by a big gray thunderbolt. Beowulf had thrown himself across the chair and locked his huge jaws on the man's upper arm. Both tumbled to the floor in a snarling pile.

"Good God!" the second man yelled from the hall and came charging in.

Packy chose that moment to make his own move. Not in the direction any of them could have anticipated. Instead he turned toward the windows, covered his face with his arms, tucked his chin down on to his breastbone, and hurled himself through the pane of glass.

"Get him!" Rolf roared. The second man rushed for the window. Maeve, frozen until that moment, stuck out her foot. The assailant tripped, slid a few feet across the floor, and slammed his head against the wall. And all this time Rob Stanley had remained fixed in position, his whole body shaking.

The man on the floor wrestling with Beowulf was losing. Those massive jaws had shifted up his arm to his shoulder, just inches away from his throat. Rolf, cursing madly, went over to the pair and kicked the dog. Beowulf paid him no attention. He had zeroed in on his target, and had no intention of giving up. Rolf picked up one of the light chairs and used it as a club to batter at the dog's head.

"Don't you touch my dog!" Maeve roared. "Rob! Make him stop."

But the big bluff man had all the responses of a bowl of jelly. He shook and quivered and a tear of frustration formed in his eye. Maeve could not wait another second. She threw her one hundred and twenty-five pounds into Rolf's stomach, much like a tackler in a football game. The man fended her off, struggled to reestablish his balance, and swung the remnants of the chair at her head. The rest was darkness.

Someone was carrying her in their arms. Her head ached massively. Her hands were tied behind her back. In front of her two men were walking carefully, carrying flat plastic-wrapped packages. The diamonds, Maeve thought as she managed to open one eye. Even in the darkness she could tell that Rob Stanley was her porter. She tried the other eye as well. He noticed her movement and looked down at her.

"Damn woman," he muttered. "Why couldn't you leave well enough alone? So you have to be a heroine, and now we're *all* in the soup."

"Beowulf," she muttered groggily. "Where's my dog?"

"Where did you expect?" he grumbled. "Rolf beat him up and they threw him in a closet. What else? Busybody. You know what your snooping has done? They're going to kill you, you stupid woman. And maybe me too. Damn you! Those uncut diamonds could be worth millions!"

"Yeah, I can see you're worried about *me*. Ash told me you'd crack one day. I should have listened."

"Women aren't too bright in any circumstances," he told her. "The world won't miss you all that much."

"This is all crazy," Maeve said, feeling a little stronger. "Smuggling where there is no harbor? Poling across the swamps? Why not use a decent port and go off in a truck?"

"Because that's what the police are looking for," he snapped. "They're blanking out the drug smuggling so well that we keep losing our diamond shipments in the middle of their nets. So we're doing the unexpected. It's all my plan, and it would have worked perfectly——"

"Until you got caught in your own trap," Maeve said. At least that's one point of satisfaction, she thought. "If only my head didn't ache so much."

"You don't have a lot of time to suffer," he muttered. "They're going to wrap a couple of rocks around you and dump you in the swamp."

"Thanks." Maeve, trying desperately to be brave, was losing the battle, but her curiosity was not yet slaked. "Packy," she asked. "Where's Packy?"

"I don't know," Stanley admitted. "The old geezer got away. Who would have thought he could move like that? God, you're heavy."

"I've been eating too much lately," she said sarcastically. "Just drop me anywhere along here. I won't mind."

"Shut up."

Nag at him, she told herself. Get him flustered. A few more steps. She could smell the swamp. He dropped her, luckily on a moss-covered bank. Her head snapped back. Poor Beowulf. All the years he had been *her* dog. She rolled over on her side and mourned. Fear of death came on strong, and made her teeth chatter.

The group was at the edge of one of the narrow swamp waterways. Flashlights were concentrated on four pirogues. The flat packages were being stored neatly in two of them. The others were for...?

"You," Rob Stanley said as he leaned over and tossed her into the bow of the boat. She landed with a thud, bruising her ribs. "Have a good trip," he said bitterly. "A last trip."

"Come with me for your own," she invited. He swore at her mightily, until Rolf appeared at his side.

"You talk too much," the man said. "You ride with her. You know how to pole, no?"

"I know how," Stanley muttered. "*She's* the one who talks too much."

"So gag her. Move."

"Move," the big blond man muttered. "I'm the boss here. I'll move when I'm ready." He reached into his pocket and pulled out a cigarette. His hands shook so much that he could hardly light the end. He inhaled strongly, filling his lungs with the smoke of it.

"I said move," Rolf snarled as he came back to them. "And put out that damn cigarette. You can see the light of it for miles, fool."

"I'm moving, I'm moving," Stanley muttered. Maeve felt the narrow boat sway as the big man climbed in.

"The cigarette," the other man insisted as he too climbed into the boat.

The executioner, Maeve told herself. For both of us. Surely Rolf can see that Stanley is a danger to them all, not a help? Dear God, I need help. I'm not ready for this. Honestly, God, if I get out of this alive I'm going to settle down in some backwater and get married and have six kids and never open my mouth to a man again! God? She sighed. *He* was undoubtedly listening; she believed that with all her heart. But if he were answering she couldn't read the message! Maybe she needed another channel. Ash? Ash Corbet? I need you, Ash. I'll scrub your floors, iron your shirts—God, my head hurts, and I'm scared!

Kneeling in front of her, with a great deal of self-pity, Rob Stanley forced her mouth open and stuffed it with a rag that might once have been white. Then he bound the gag in place with the kerchief he wore around his neck. In order to do the work he had laid his cigarette down on the thwart between himself and Maeve, and apparently forgotten it. Now he picked up the long pole and began to push their boat away from the dry land. They were the last boat in the line of four, all moving through the darkness like a chain of alligators, heading eastward.

"Lucky," Rolf muttered from the back of the boat. "Listen." Maeve strained her ears. The night sounds of the swamp were being preempted by the scream of sirens in the distance. "We just got away in time," the small man whispered. "Somebody has information about us, no? This whole plan blows up in our face. You, Stanley, you're the boss, no? Somebody will say something in Mozambique. Pole, man."

"I'm poling," Rob Stanley said with injured dignity. "I'm poling."

"Try a little prayer, also," Rolf suggested. "Always it is good for the soul, prayer. Back home I go to church—well, not every week. That woman is gagged?"

"Gagged," Stanley agreed. Almost well enough to choke to death, Maeve thought as she stared back the length of the boat. In the distance, filtering through the swamp brush, there were flashes of light. She was hardly an eighth of a mile away from rescue. If only she... There was a closer light. The cigarette on the thwart was still alight. Not flaming, but glowing. What can I do with one cigarette?

Her tired mind struggled with the problem. She listened to the plop of sound as Stanley pulled his pole free from the bottom and got ready for another stroke. But there was another plopping sound too, not related to the boat or its movement. Sound. Where? Vague memories filtered to the fore. That day when they were stopped on the swamp road with a flat tire. Remember that, Maeve McCormac? And you lit a cigarette and snapped it out into the channel, where the methane gas was bubbling madly away? "And you can almost set the whole river on fire," Packy had said!

Packy, cigarette, river, methane. Her brain strung all the words together like a string of beans, and added one more. Luck. She had no idea where the gas was bubbling. Somewhere near by. God? Here?

She moved her foot cautiously, up to the thwart, over next to the still-burning cigarette. *Now!* something in her brain yelled at her. She kicked viciously, ignoring the pain as a sliver of wood stuck into the ball of her foot. And the lit cigarette went over the side just as a massive bubble of methane gas burst beside the wooden pirogue.

CHAPTER NINE

OUT of the darkness behind them Maeve heard the most welcome sound in the world. Well, actually the second most. A great baying howl as Beowulf exulted in his tracking signal. Somewhere out in that swamp behind them the huge old dog was on her trail. And perhaps not alone? The pirogue rocked madly, bringing her attention back to her own plight.

In all the excitement Rob Stanley had lost his pole. Maeve, startled by the result of her little ploy, managed to sit up. The cigarette had fallen at just the right place and the right time. The methane bubble had burst, flooding the night with its stench. The cigarette butt, still lit, had fallen in a graceful arc down into the concentration of gas, and the whole had exploded into flame just as the stern of the pirogue passed over it. At the stern of the pirogue, where Rolf was sitting. In the excitement Maeve lost all her fears. Action swept all else aside.

Rolf screamed. The flames had almost ignited in his face as he'd turned to look back toward the police noises. The right sleeve of his coat caught fire immediately. He screamed again as he tried madly to beat out the flames. The pirogue was old, and the sides above the watermark were dry and rotting. When the fire hit the wood it immediately burst into flame. The rear of the boat, now sitting still in the water with nobody poling, was totally aflame and sinking by the stern. Rolf was a pillar of fire, his jacket and trousers all burning madly. He gave one more scream and jumped overboard, head first.

That was probably his last mistake. The water was less than a foot deep. His dive smashed him against the accumulated debris and knocked him out. Watching his body float with the current, facedown, was too much for Maeve's sensibilities. She hated the man, feared him, but could not stand by and watch him drown. Struggling to her feet without the use of her hands was awkward.

"Sit down!" Rob Stanley yelled at her. It was a high, harsh yell; the man was almost out of control. Ignoring him, Maeve continued the struggle. The pirogue shifted and swayed as she managed to get to her feet. At the same time Stanley, his eyes blinded by fear and tears, tried desperately to snatch up his long pole. The big blond was no longer the amiable man she had known. His face was discolored with panic. He had known that he too was to be numbered among the victims of this trip. When the chief smuggler went over the side Rob felt an instant of gratification; but now he was back in the real world again—somebody was pursuing just around the bend behind them. And there was Mary Kennedy, the only witness. He managed to get both hands around the grip of the pole and turned around in the boat.

His movement was just what was needed. The pirogue gurgled to itself and settled on the bottom, sending up a cloud of pollution that had probably rested in place for years. Maeve, watching Stanley and the end of that heavy pole which moved in her direction, stepped out of the boat and into the shallows. The pirogue, its weight redistributed, rose in the bows. Stanley was thrown completely off balance, and he, pole and all, went over the side in a flat dive that sent a resounding splat through the night.

Rolf, still unconscious, floated by Maeve's legs. She turned around to hook his shirt in her still-tied hands, and flipped him over onto his back. He promptly ran aground and lay still, his head above water.

But this last impulse was too much for Maeve's footing. She slipped, tottered, and went down in the muck. It was almost impossible for her to recover. She rolled over, coating herself with more mud, and managed to scrabble up on to her knees, but more than that was beyond her. And at that moment the light from a powerful flashlight swept across her and focused on Rob Stanley. He had managed to grab some of the nearby brush, and had pulled himself up. Maeve tried her best to scream a warning, but the gag in her mouth made that all but impossible.

The police boat, with two men poling at top speed, came down on the motley crew of disorganized smugglers at full speed. Maeve ducked her head to wash the mud out of her eyes, and then watched as the light pinned Stanley in position.

"Don't move a finger!"

Maeve managed a breath through clogged nostrils, and mentally relaxed. Ash had come for her, and the world was about to become right again. All her fears vanished in that one moment. All the terror of Rolf's threats, all the weaknesses of Rob Stanley, all disappeared, banished forever. Or so she thought at that moment.

Instead of remaining in place, Rob Stanley, slipping and sliding, tried to pull himself up on a hummock of dry ground, and in so doing he slid into Maeve and knocked her down into the mud again. The police came out of their boat in a rush, cavorting like a band of gypsy dancers on a slick floor.

"It was an accident!" Stanley screamed at them. "I——"

"Just stay where the hell you are!" Ash Corbet was on him at that moment. Rob Stanley had no intention of moving, but his feet slipped again and he smashed into Corbet and almost put them both in the muck.

"Where is she?" Before Stanley could answer, Corbet's fist came back and slammed into Stanley's stomach. The big man bent over in agony. "Where is she?" Another fist to the jaw straightened the blond up again. A second police boat appeared on the scene.

"Don't hit him again, for God's sake," Ralph Wilson yelled as he grappled with Ash. "He's had it."

By this time Maeve had come back up out of the water, and was once again struggling to get to her knees. Nobody paid her any attention at all. Not only was she coated solidly black, but she was tired, worn beyond comprehension and, more than that, her Irish dander was rising like a runaway thermometer. If *anyone* had looked at her, come to her, said a nice word, she would have rioted with joy. But to have *nothing* happen? That was just too much. You can't, she told herself firmly, love a man every minute of the day, can you?

"Listen!" Ash yelled. "Take one boat and go after them. There has to be another—maybe two boats still ahead of us. Watch for this Rolf fellow. And most of all watch for my girl!"

"Here. Over here," Maeve tried to yell, but the gag was not only effective, it had absorbed a considerable amount of swamp water, which was trickling down her throat. The manned boat went by her with a rush. With no other means of signaling, Maeve wiggled back and forth.

"Something over here," one of the men yelled from the departing boat. "Watch it. It might be a 'gator."

"That's all we need," Ash Corbet grumbled. "Miss all the smugglers, lose my girl, and now an alligator!" He swung the beam of his big flashlight around until it pinpointed Maeve. Still on her knees, totally plastered with mud and grime, she looked more like a 'gator than a girl.

"What the hell is it?" Ash asked. There was a clattering overhead. The police helicopter had arrived on the scene. The two massive spotlights on the aircraft lit up the swamp like a movie set. "My God!" Ash Corbet roared as he abandoned his captive and plowed through the shallow water. "Mae? Is that you, Mae?"

Tired but relieved, even happy, Maeve sank back on her haunches and tried her best to mumble a word or two. Nothing came out. His hands reached down under her armpits and pulled her to her feet. She leaned against him for strength. "What the hell have they done to you?" he muttered as his hands found the ropes around her wrists. He whirled her around and tried the knots with one hand, the other still holding the flashlight.

"Here's that Mozambique guy," one of his assistants called. "Out cold. What do you——?"

"Put him in the bloody boat," Ash snarled. Maeve, still behind her mask of mud and muck, could tell that his anger was rising. So how about me? she thought. I could use a little Tender Loving Care, a little appreciation! The knots slipped, and her hands came free. She pulled them around in front of her, chafing at the wrists to restore circulation. One more pull and Ash turned her around to face him. In the light of the flashlight she looked as if she were wearing a mudpack.

"Mae?" he asked. "Are you still mad at me about all this undercover stuff I've had to perform?"

Maeve tried her best to reassure him, but her best was not good enough. The gag was covered with mud; she knew he probably could not see it, but it hardly made her feel any better. The kerchief that held it in place was knotted behind her head, but her arms were too weak to reach those knots.

"Dear God, Mae," he said. "Don't treat me like this. I love you!"

"What do I do with these two?" one of the policemen asked.

"I don't give a damn!" Ash snapped. "Dump them in the swamp. I just don't—— Mae?" She was doing her best to demonstrate what the problem was. He was a slow learner. And now, very slowly, Maeve McCormac began to realize how ridiculous their situation was. They were standing in a foot of water in the middle of the Suwannee swamps, she covered with mud, and he almost pristine clean, and he wanted to tell her that he... All of a sudden it became hilarious.

"Mae? You're making funny noises." Gathering up her strength she lifted one of his hands and placed it where her mouth ought to be. "Oh, my God," the chief law-enforcement officer of Dixie County said. It seemed to be his favorite expression, Maeve told herself. But now he had the problem in hand.

Once again the knots were slippery. He fumbled with them, not too gently, until finally they came apart and she was able to spit out the rag stuffed in her mouth. She coughed violently, and sniffed a couple of times, then collapsed against his chest again. "Mae?"

"I'm all right." She wasn't. She hawked and cleared her throat, then repeated her statement.

"The hell you are!" he roared at her.

"Hey," she roared back. "I'm the victim in this darn crime! What took you so long?"

"I came as fast as I could," he snarled at her. "Crazy woman. Did you think you could capture the whole gang of them all by yourself? Crazy!"

"I wasn't all by myself," she returned. "I had Beowulf and Packy. Oh, my, Beowulf—is he——?"

"No, he isn't dead. The bullet just creased his skull and knocked him out. And as for Packy, he——"

"He's a wonderful man," she sighed. "If he were sixty years younger I'd marry him. A wonderful——"

"Will you shut up?"

"Well, you don't have to be so nerdy about things. I was only——"

"I said shut up!" Less than a quarter of a mile away the sounds of the helicopters rose to a crescendo, and captured their attention for a moment. The searchlights even lit up their small section of swamp. There was the sound of an amplified voice from the air, and eventually the radio in one of the policemen's pockets rattled and spat out something worthwhile.

"They've got the other boats," the officer reported. "I sure would like to get the hell out of here. Could I put these men in the boat and take them back?"

"I've got more important things to worry about," Ash told him, and then turned back to Maeve.

"You're some sort of a dictator," she snapped at him.

"That's right," he agreed. "Now, listen up."

There was a moment's silence while she thought and he watched. And then, "Mary Kennedy, will you marry me?"

"I—what?" That last rose to a screech that put the helicopters to shame. And then, more softly. "What did you say?"

"I said, will you marry me? For better, for worse, in madness or in pleasure. Will you?"

"That isn't the way the line goes," she protested, stalling for time. Marry him? Till death do us part? What kind of a fool would turn down an offer like *that*? So we're not sitting on the couch sipping wine and eating crumb cakes—and maybe we'll never own a couch, or have a chance to...and then there'll be children, and I

could love him and them all through my life, and
blackmail him forever by telling the kids about how he
proposed to me...

"I'm sorry I didn't bring a ring," Ash added. "Well?"

"Forever's a long time," she said very meekly. There
was the need to do feminine things. Run a hand through
her mud-clogged hair. Straighten her blouse. Look up
at him. Although his flashlight was on her, she could
see his face. Immaculate, almost, except for a spot of
mud right on the tip of his nose. She stretched up to
brush it off, but her fingers had more of the muck than
his nose did, and she only managed to spread the spot.

"Take a chance," he suggested hopefully. "Yes or
yes?"

"Why—of course I will," she said, trying to smile.
He bent down and shared the junk that covered her lips.
It was almost a kiss.

"Thank God!" he said. To him, she knew, it was only
an exclamation. To her there was a great need to do just
that.

She bowed her head and whispered, "Thank you,
God," and her heart soared.

"And don't worry about a diamond ring," she teased.
"I brought one with me. Or, to tell the truth, perhaps
five hundred of them. We could take our pick." Ash
looked down at her, mouth open. He tried vainly to brush
her hair back off her face. And then he smiled.

"You mean that's what they were smuggling?
Diamonds?"

"Exactly," she bragged. "And I broke up the ring
and captured them all!"

"Not exactly all," he said. "There are still a couple
up-river you didn't manage to catch." He pulled her
closer, mud and all. "And there's nothing worse than a
bragging wife," he whispered.

It all sounded so nice. *Wife!* "So you helped," she whispered back. He added one more muddy hug. His teeth were showing white in the darkness, so he must have been smiling in return.

"Now," he said loudly, "let's get everybody back to the settlement."

"And it's about damn time," the big policeman who had been holding Rolf's head up out of the water said.

"And just to prove how much I love you," Ash told Maeve rather pompously, "I'm going to carry you over to the boat."

"I—wouldn't do that," Maeve protested, but her Lochinvar was already at work. He swung her up into his arms and stood there for a moment as she dripped in various places. "I wouldn't do that," Maeve repeated as he took a tentative step in the direction of the boat. And then his foot slipped. He teetered for a moment. Maeve squealed. And they both landed in the deepest part of the channel, amid the biggest pile of muck and mud there was available.

"I knew we should have gone earlier," the braver policeman commented as he pushed Rob Stanley back toward the boat.

But the chief law-enforcement officer of Dixie County was sitting in water up to—well, higher than that, and glaring down at his recently affianced bride, who was laughing her fool head off, and smearing those portions of his face not yet covered with the concoction she had been wearing for some time.

CHAPTER TEN

THE police car delivered them to her door just two hours before sunrise, and then roared off with the prisoners. Maeve was beginning to feel like a well-preserved cake, soft on the inside, solid dried mud-brown on the outside. It hurt to smile. And she had hardly the nerve to look up at her companion.

Somehow, in the enthusiasm of the night, Ash Corbet had lost his outward veneer of casual attraction. He looked about like a bagman on the streets of Chicago. But if you love him as he is, Maeve assured herself, then there are bound to be endless wonderful days ahead of us!

"You look terrible, but I love you just the same," she told him.

"Something around here smells awful," he countered as he put a companionable arm around her shoulders and ushered her into the house. "First dibs on the showers?"

"Women and children first," she stated firmly. "The ancient law of the sea."

"Well, this ancient lawyer can't wait," he protested. "I'd have thought you'd be nice to me. I *did* get your dog to the veterinarian, didn't I? That took a lot of influence at this time of night."

Maeve stifled a giggle. "And that veterinarian didn't even know who you were," she told him. "And he's the one you went to school with all those years."

"Twelve years," he admitted dolefully. "Best buddies."

"It *was* a fine thing you did," she said. "So... I have a fairly big shower stall. Why don't we——?"

"Share! What a marvelous idea," he interrupted. "Lead the way. I seem to have something stuck in my eye." He made a vague wave in the direction of that orb.

Maeve was glad her face was not on view. She could feel the blush forming. Hidden behind one thin coat of mud she had thrown off all her inhibitions, but with the shield washed away? She reached for his hand and towed him after her, down the corridor to the bathroom. It hardly seemed the time to stand on formality. The shower water steamed and filled the room with mist as she quickly stripped, and then stood watching as he did the same.

"Why, you aren't *all* mud," he commented as one of his hands crossed the space between them and gently touched her breast. Her unwarned nipple sprang to attention.

"And neither are you," she sighed happily. "I've never—you..." and words failed her entirely as she hurried into the cubicle and plunged under the welcoming water.

He came in directly behind her, but as the mud slowly washed away she hadn't the courage to turn around and face him. In a moment his hands, washed clean, were on her back, massaging with the aloe soap she favored. Around and around, in sensitive circles, those hands moved. High up on her shoulders, then down to the middle of her back, then down further, to the swell of her pert little bottom. And all the time he kept up a line of inconsequential chatter that tickled her fancy as much as his hands were arousing her libido.

"Lovely back," he crooned. "Not a mark anywhere. Just a little too much flesh over here? We'll have to find something to keep my little lady in better shape. And what is this lovely——?"

She laughed as she slapped his hand away from the forward curve of her hip. "My hair's a mess," she complained. But he wasn't interested in hair. His hands came around her, still covered with lather, and began to march up and down from her navel to her breasts. Gently, tenderly, flamingly! There's no such word as that! her practical mind assured her. Calm down! Hair. Shampoo.

He had the plastic bottle in his hands before she could say a word. It was what she wanted. What she needed. But she hated it when his hands gave up their assault and moved up to her head. Teasing, she told herself. He's a tease. Why do I love it so much? By that time he'd pushed her under the shower head and was rinsing away, singing one of those Walt Disney songs about dwarfs and "Heigh ho" and foolish things of that nature. But at last she was clean, gloriously clean. Tired but clean.

"What——?"

"Stand still. Now it's my turn," she commanded as she seized the soap bar and moved behind him.

"Nothing I hate worse than a dominating woman," he complained dolefully, but obeyed none the less. Her hands were hard at work, but his muscles were like rock. There was no give as she applied her maximum strength.

"Relax," she commanded as her tired arms moved down to his hips and around to his front.

"You've got to be kidding, lady," he replied caustically. "Relax?"

"I—— Oh." She had just discovered why he couldn't relax. Her hands withdrew of their own volition. "I'm sorry."

"Well, I'm not," he said over his shoulder. "You can do that as much as you like—but I'm a long way from home and need a bed for the night."

"I have a king-size bed," she offered, and then almost bit her tongue as he swung around, gathered her up in his arms, and held her with considerable fervor.

"Now we're talking about bed sharing?"

"I—it seemed the only companionable thing to do," she said. "What with your saving my life and all. You did mean that, about marriage, and all that?"

"Don't ever doubt it," he said, chuckling, as he carried her out of the shower and wrapped her up in one of her enormous bath-towels. "Which way to the bedroom?"

She told him, and it was the only direction he required for the remainder of the night.

Maeve awoke slowly. She had heard the telephone ring, and ignored it. But when the massive warmth against which she was cuddled moved away she was instantly lonely. And moments later, as she heard the drone of the conversation continue, it could no longer be ignored. She opened one eye. Ash was gone. Maeve stretched, like a huge cat who had spent the whole night at the cream dish. Entirely satisfactory, she told herself. Entirely. It had been *much* better than she had dreamed it could be. A wicked little grin teased her face. And here I am, she told herself, and there is Ash Corbet, at the telephone, talking to my——

"Oh, my goodness. Talking to my mother!"

"Ah, Lady Bountiful is awake?" He stuck his head in the bedroom, telephone still at hand. "Mrs. McCormac, I believe lovable little Mae has finally awakened." He handed over the telephone, and, while she talked, twisted a finger in her auburn curls. A most annoying habit that she could come to love, she knew.

She tried with one hand to pull her nightgown on. Somehow it had landed on the floor during the night. His helping hand brushed against several parts of her anatomy that ached. She fumbled for her robe to cover herself.

"Mamma? Mamma, I'm going to be married!"

"Well, I should hope so, love. The nice young man said he'd spent the night with you!" Which gave Maeve an altogether new slant on things. She had never really thought of Ash Corbet as being a "nice young man." In fact, even before the events of the past twenty-four hours, he intimidated her. Just the slightest, of course, but there it was with no bark on it.

"I—yes," she sighed down the telephone line. "It's been a difficult night, too lengthy to explain on a long-distance telephone call, so I——"

"Then you can tell me when he brings you up here for the wedding," her mother replied, and Maeve could hear the laughter. Her *own* mother, laughing at her!

"I—didn't know we were coming up to Apalachicola for the wedding," she mumbled.

"I see. One of those dominating men?"

"Oh, Mother!"

"Yes, well, call when he gives you the details," her mother laughed as she hung up. Maeve turned to Ash, just the tiniest bit angry about the whole affair.

"You told my mother?"

"It seemed like the proper thing to do," he returned. "I couldn't think of a quick excuse for having spent the night in your bed. Mothers are sensitive about things like that." His solemn face haunted her; she ducked her head.

"You never thought I might like to have something to say about it?"

"Of course I did, Maeve McCormac," he said, chuckling. "Only you were asleep. Don't you want to go up to Apalachicola with me and get married?"

"That's a package deal? Go up there and get married?"

"A package deal." And for just a second she could see a look of doubt and anxiety peeping out of the corner of those dark eyes of his. "Well?"

"I'm thinking," she told him.

"The offer's only good for a limited time," he replied. "Well?"

"I'll take it, I'll take it," she hurried to say. "But don't think you can spend the rest of your life lording it over me, Ashton Corbet!" And just saying his name alerted her sleepy mind. Yes, she told herself, he *is* a large dominating man, who means to get his own way come hell or high water, and he called me—Maeve McCormac. Oh, Lord!

She felt with one hand blindly for the brass knob on the bed, and guided herself over to plump down on the mattress. "Why did you call me that?"

"Maeve McCormac? Because that's your name," he said. "I'm not going to marry you under false pretenses."

"My mother told you?"

"No. Your fingerprints told me."

And now we *really* have to talk, she told herself as the mattress sank under his weight and his arm came around her shoulders. Keep your head down, and don't look at him, she commanded herself. "What fingerprints?"

"The ones on your coffee mug," he said in a very self-satisfied tone of voice. "I read about that in a 'How To Be A Detective' book I bought."

"Nonsense." It was hard to be placid about the whole affair. He knew too much. Her whole new identity was about to be destroyed! "I wish Packy were here."

"Now *that's* nonsense," he agreed. "He was by earlier, flying over the rainbow. Five hundred of those bottles of wine were still good. I threw the old pack rat out on his ear."

"He was very good to me." Another thought flashed through her mind. "You couldn't have identified me," she stated very firmly. "I don't have my prints on record any place."

"Well, how about that," he murmured. "You forget. You enlisted your dog in the army, remember? They didn't fingerprint the dog; they printed you. Are you denying it, Maeve?"

"Does it matter?" She was suddenly tired, worn to the bone. The wild night of fear and frustration, the early morning induction into womanhood, and now this—collapse of her last barrier. His arm tightened around her shoulders, and he squeezed gently.

"I'm going to marry you, even if your name is Mata Hari," he said. That deep soft voice comforted her. She shivered and then moved closer to him. He added a kiss to the tip of her little button nose. "But you're going to have to give up this detecting business. One of us in the law is enough. So you solved Packy's problem——"

"Purely by accident," she muttered.

"Whatever. And then you solved the smuggling problem for us."

"Yes; I thought *you* were the smuggler," she admitted.

"No matter. The county is going to make a bundle out of this. We get to confiscate Stanley's house, his business, and all those stacks of computer equipment. No wonder he didn't want you exploring his house. You startled him, wanting to visit his mother. He shipped her out of here fast enough to work up a wind storm! But that's the ever-loving end. No more, y'hear?"

"I hear, but there's something more I need to tell you," she confessed as she turned into him and buried her head against his bare chest.

"I thought there might be," he chuckled.

"But first you need to answer a question or two," she added very firmly.

"I knew it was going too easy," he said. "Fire away."

"You're really the county attorney?"

"I really am," he admitted. "But I've only had the job for about a month."

"Then how come nobody in the Cove knew who you were?"

"Because I received a special appointment to the post," he assured her. "In camera, as the Pope would say."

"In secret? And now? Can you——?"

"Yes, I can support a wife—and her dog——"

"And six children?" she interjected. His big finger tilted her head up to where he could look into her green eyes.

"And six children," he said. "But not all at once?"

"Whenever," she sighed and snuggled up against him again. "Now I think I'd better tell you about Uncle Shamus."

It was a long story, but it rolled out at flank speed, and towards the end he was laughing.

"It isn't all that funny," she declared indignantly. And just at that moment a car pulled up outside the house, and someone was knocking on the front door.

Ash stretched upward and took a quick look out of the window. "Duty calls," he said.

"I have to get dressed," she told him.

"It would be a complete waste of time, Maeve. Just fasten up your robe, like so." He did all the buttons, lingering perhaps a little too long at the pair at her bodice. And she loved it. "After I settle this fellow's hash, we'll have a nice breakfast—which I will cook—or we'll go back to bed," he said.

"I'd like that," she told him wistfully. "Either one. Or both?" So Maeve followed him out of the bedroom, wondering what had happened to all her years of Calvinist upbringing. All gone, every little strain, every little quibble, every little Biblical quotation. Except one. "Whither thou goest," she quoted under her breath, and hurried to catch up.

There were three men in her kitchen. Two very large policemen, and one very rotund and shaking little villain, Uncle Shamus McCormac.

"He calls himself McCormac," one of the policemen reported. "We picked him up just the way you expected, at the best hotel and in the best suite in the state. Says he's a real-estate man."

"And I surely do not understand why all this harassment," Uncle Shamus said as he drew himself up in all his dignity. "Snatched out of my hotel room like some common criminal! My Congressman will hear about this. What's the charge? I insist on knowing what the charge is!"

"I'm not sure exactly," Ash said as he guided Maeve to a chair. "How about grand larceny. Or forgery. Or—say, how about murder?"

"Murder?" The little man squealed like a stuck pig. "I—no, that's not possible!"

"No? Then where is the body of Maeve McCormac?"

"Body? I——"

"You say she's dead," Ash went on inexorably. "So if she's dead there must be a body. Where did you hide it?"

"I——" The little man gulped. "Murder? You can't prove murder. I—can you?"

"Easy enough," Ash assured him. "We don't actually need a body. *Corpus delicti* refers to the body of the crime, not the body of the victim. And we can certainly prove that out of your own mouth, Mr. McCormac." A moment of silence, while the little man's Adam's apple bobbed up and down. And then the hook. "Unless you would want to help us by pleading guilty to some lesser charge and making restitution?"

Like a trout rising to the fly, the little man bit. "Yes. Lord, yes." He wiped his forehead. "I'll tell you anything you want to know. But not about murder. I never murdered Maeve McCormac. Honestly! Can I sit down?"

He slumped into the nearest kitchen chair. "I never murdered the girl," he said softly. "I'm really a sort of uncle to her, you know. Her father was my third cousin."

"Then let me introduce you," Ash said in that kindly authoritative voice, the one that might well charm birds down from the trees. Maeve pinched herself in warning. Some day he might want to try that line out on *her*, and it was obvious that if she was to survive in a marriage to this man she needed to have a thousand preplanned defenses!

Ash waved his arm in Maeve's direction. "This is my future wife, Maeve McCormac."

"Oh, God." Her would-be uncle slumped even more. "I never really meant to do you any harm," he said, sighing. "I was always jealous of your father. He made money hand over fist, and I—never had the success he did. Until I thought about this—confidence game. At first it was only a game. I enjoyed the playing of it more than the money. And then the money went to my head, the game got more complicated, and I just couldn't stop. It became an addiction. I'm that sorry, lass. Forgive me."

"She could be a lot more forgiving if you made some restitution," Ash interjected. "What have you done with all the money?"

"In an account at the First Federal in Baton Rouge, Louisiana," Uncle Shamus said. "Almost all of it. I used a—fairly large sum for living expenses. Almost a quarter of a million dollars. God, it's fun to live rich. I didn't realize how fast it was going out."

"And you sold all the property?"

"No, not all of it," the old man confessed. "There's still all the land here, and some outside of Apalachicola, and a large tract in Atlanta."

"All sold for what—ten cents on the dollar?"

"Something like that. They all knew they were handling—a peculiar property sale. I don't suppose you could get any of it back?"

"It would take years," Ash admitted. "But she has a good lawyer, and he's willing to try."

"I have?" He was standing beside her chair. Maeve leaned over against his thigh and looked up at him.

"The best in all Florida," he said, chuckling. "Me."

"Then—if he gives me all the money," she continued thoughtfully, "and all the papers for the remaining land...I really don't want to prosecute, Ash." She took another quick peep up at him. He frowned down at her.

"Is that the *only* reason you don't want to prosecute, because he's some relative of yours?"

"Not really." Maeve's eyes clung to his face as she talked, so softly that he had to strain his ears to hear. "No. It's because—if I hadn't come to the Cove chasing Uncle Shamus, I would never have met you!" His rocky face disintegrated into a smile, which gave her courage enough to continue. "And *then*, after all, he *is* my uncle—after a fashion. Nobody wants to put their uncle in jail."

"And that is probably the best offer you're ever going to get," Ash said. "Pay-up time, Uncle Shamus."

"Yes. Yes, indeed," the man babbled. "Yes!" He reached into his coat pocket and pulled out a checkbook. His pen scratched across a blank. He tore it out of the book and handed it over. Maeve stared at it; it was a very respectable sum. She looked up at Ash with a question in her eyes. He grinned down at her.

"It will do," he told her. "But just barely. Six children can be very expensive. You're a very lucky man, Uncle Shamus. Not many nieces would be as nice as this one. Now, just to make sure that nobody calls this bank and stops action on the check, why don't you go back to Cross City for a few days with my friends here? The county will provide a place for you to stay. While you're waiting for the check to clear you can write out a complete explanation of the whole affair. We'd call it a confession if you were going to be charged with anything. And who knows——?"

"I wouldn't think of anything underhand," Uncle Shamus babbled.

"I hope you wouldn't," Ash said grimly. "Off you go."

"I know it sounds silly," Maeve interjected, "but I'd like to invite my uncle to my wedding. He's the only male relative I've got."

"Well, I'll be——" Ash snorted.

"Probably," his future wife assured him. She had found the answer to a happy married life. Keep him off balance! She stood up and put her arm around his waist as the two policemen escorted her uncle out into the police car.

"Cruel," Maeve said moodily as she rested both elbows on the kitchen table. "You were cruel to him."

"You would rather have done it some other way?"

"Yes." She brightened up perceptibly. "Before I heard his side of the story I would have preferred chaining him in a dungeon or something! Now, about my dog?"

"Your dog is fine," he assured her. "I called the vet."

"I need to hear that firsthand," she insisted, pushing herself away from the table.

"That's not on the menu," he said as he loomed over her. "Breakfast or...?"

She grinned mischievously up at him as he swept her up in his arms. "Okay," she surrendered, knowing when she was thoroughly beaten. "I'll take the 'or...' if you think you can handle it?"

He growled down at her and carried her away to the bedroom. "I'll show you who can handle it!"

"I might like that," Maeve McCormac said with enthusiasm, knowing there was no "might" at all involved in the situation. "And *then* I'll call about my dog!"

But as he tossed her none too gently on to the bed Maeve knew in a flash that Beowulf would *certainly* need an extra day or two at the kennel, so she stretched up her arms eagerly toward her man, and giggled as he fumbled and cursed at the buttons of her robe, which he had so skillfully fastened not more than an hour ago.

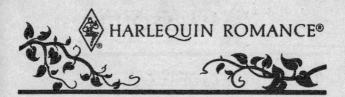

HARLEQUIN ROMANCE®

**Harlequin Romance
knows love can be dangerous!**

Don't miss
TO LOVE AND PROTECT (#3223)
by Kate Denton,
the October title in

THE BRIDAL COLLECTION

THE GROOM'S life was in peril.
THE BRIDE was hired to help him.
BUT THEIR WEDDING was *more* than
a business arrangement!

Available this month in
The Bridal Collection
JACK OF HEARTS (#3218)
by Heather Allison

Wherever Harlequin books are sold.

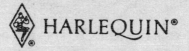 **HARLEQUIN®**

THE TAGGARTS OF TEXAS!

Harlequin's Ruth Jean Dale brings you
THE TAGGARTS OF TEXAS!

Those Taggart men—strong, sexy and hard to resist...

You've met Jesse James Taggart in FIREWORKS!
Harlequin Romance #3205 (July 1992)

Now meet Trey Smith—he's THE RED-BLOODED YANKEE!
Harlequin Temptation #413 (October 1992)

Then there's Daniel Boone Taggart in SHOWDOWN!
Harlequin Romance #3242 (January 1993)

And finally the Taggarts who started it all—in LEGEND!
Harlequin Historical #168 (April 1993)

Read all the Taggart romances!
Meet all the Taggart men!

Available wherever Harlequin books are sold.